"Reading Kim Magowan's story collection, *Undoing,* is like viewing a series of X-rays on a lightboard—over and over we're offered a glin surface that men and into the murky, moral spots grow otherwise u overpopulated by doon what raises Magowan's afflicted characters far above this legion of the walking dead is that they manage to carry on despite the secrets eating away inside them. With humor, insight, and brutal honesty, they confront head-on the frightening, unadvertised realization that no one person can truly complete us."

—**Chris Belden, author of** *Shriver* **and**
The Floating Lady of Lake Tawaba

"I literally felt undone reading Kim Magowan's *Undoing.* Though a work of fiction, the poet in me was left hanging at the edge of most lines. A beautiful book that felt like existing inside a dream for the pleasurable hours it took me to wind my way through the surreal treatment of relationships."

—**Suzanne Burns, author of**
The Veneration of Monsters

"Precise prose, characters cartwheeling into and around each other, *Undoing* is about doing, and Kim Magowan's writing doesn't mess around. An interesting, provocative read, where every word counts."

—**Kim Chinquee, author of**
Oh Baby **and** *Shot Girls*

UNDOING

KIM MAGOWAN

Moon City Press

MOON CITY PRESS
Department of English
Missouri State University
901 South National Avenue
Springfield, Missouri 65897

First Edition
Copyright © 2018 by Kim Magowan
All rights reserved.
Published by Moon City Press, Springfield, Missouri, USA, in 2018.

Library of Congress Cataloging-in-Publication Data

Magowan, Kim.
Undoing: stories/Kim Magowan, 1967–

2018935005

Further Library of Congress information is available upon request.

ISBN-10: 0-913785-78-4
ISBN-13: 978-0-913785-78-2

Cover and interior designed by Charli Barnes

Edited by Joel Coltharp & Michael Czyzniejewski
Text copyedited by Karen Craigo

Manufactured in the United States of America.

moon-city-press.com

ACKNOWLEDGEMENTS

Thank you very much to the team at Moon City Press, especially Michael Czyniejewski, Joel Coltharp, and Karen Craigo, for their dedication to this book and the care they have taken to usher it into the world. Thank you, Charli Barnes, for designing its beautiful, eerie cover.

Thank you, Molly Antopol, Chris Belden, Suzanne Burns, Kim Chinquee, Jac Jemc, and Adam Johnson. The generous praise of these writers I so admire undoes me.

Thank you to all the editors over the years who have picked my stories from slush piles. Special thanks to those editors who have been particularly supportive and whose judicious cuts and smart suggestions have made my stories better: Lenae Souza Crowder, Mark Drew, Chris Frakes, Andrea Gregory, Christopher Morgan, Sahar Mustafah, Peter Stitt, and Laura Zink.

Thank you to my colleagues at Mills College who read early drafts of these stories: Diane Cady, Achy Obejas, Sarah Pollock, Kirsten Saxton, Thomas Strychacz, and Kara Wittman.

Thank you to all my students, over the years, who have taught me so much about words, writing, and being human. I am proud of the former students who have become writers and editors themselves, whom I share space with in literary journals. I am especially grateful to the ones who workshopped drafts of many of the stories in this book: Michael Canterino, Sarah Hoenicke, Alexandra Kamerling, Aliza Rood, Cassidy Smith, and Rebecca Vicino.

Thank you to my friends who have read my fiction over the past three decades, including early iterations barely recognizable here: Kristin Barendsen, Chris Belden, Susie Britton, Robert Chihade, Cynthia Dobbs, Daniel Garvin, Jerome Gentes, Jennifer Granick, Elaine Greco, Dorothy Hale, Randy Kline, Robert Landon, Ronald Loewinsohn, Jennifer Lynch, Yasmina Din Madden, Robin Magowan, Anton Malko, George Malko, Jeffrey McCarthy, Aimee Mepham, Mark Phillipson, Alexandra Quinn, Anne Raeff, Jennifer Reese, David Robinson, Karie Rubin, Traci Shafroth, Mark Smoyer, Dana Stevens, Tamara Straus, Emily Kaiser Thelin, Elizabeth Weil, Robert Weinstock, and Mark Yakich.

A particular thank you to Michelle Ross, who has read every story here, some in ugly, newborn condition; who helps me prune similes and trim the fat; who solves such murky riddles as the proper sequence of stories in a collection; who motivates and inspires me. For every writer, I wish a first reader as judicious as Michelle. I'll always be grateful to *Sixfold* for connecting us. This is a better book because of her.

Thank you to my family, who have indulged and nurtured me as a writer since I was a kid bouncing a ball and telling myself (very loud) stories: my sister, Margot Magowan, for years my first reader; my sister, Hilary Magowan, my unofficial publicist; my father, Peter Magowan, who spams his friends and relatives with my stories; my mother, Jill Oriane Tarlau, who fixes my commas and deletes extra adverbs, and who instilled in me a love of words.

Thank you to my partner, Bryan Wagner, who had faith that this book would materialize when I had my doubts and who is always honest with me about which stories work best. He is the reader whose opinion I most value. I could not have written this book without his support and love.

Finally, thank you to my daughters, Nora and Camille, for entertaining, stretching, and inspiring me, for handing me more than one title, and for letting me steal some of their lines.

The author would like to thank the editors of the following journals, where the listed stories have originally appeared:

"When in Rome" *JMMW* (March 11, 2015) (published under the title "Undoing")

"Why We Are With the Men We Are With" *Hobart* (February 3, 2016); republished in *The Literary Review Share* (September 14, 2016)

"Eleanor of Aquitaine" *Bird's Thumb* Volume 2 Issue 3 (October 2015)

"Warmer, Colder" *Word Riot* (June 2015)

"Buko" *Corium Magazine* Issue 20 (Summer 2015)

"Brining" *Sixfold* (Winter 2015)

"Palimpsest" *Indiana Review* Volume 33 Number 2 (Winter 2011)

"On Air" *Bird's Thumb* Volume 3 Issue 2 (June 2016)

"Wheels Inside Wheels" *New World Writing* (April 2, 2017)

"Tabloid" *River City* Volume 21 Issue 2 (Summer 2001)

"Be Good" *Fiction Southeast* (May 26, 2016)

"Nepenthes" *decomP magazinE* (October 4 1017)

"Version" *The Gettysburg Review* Volume 24 Number 4 (Winter 2011)

"Mrs. White in the Ballroom with the Lead Pipe" *Fiction Southeast* (August 22, 2015)

"Sugarman" *Squalorly* (Summer 2015)

"640" *Fiction Southeast* (November 17, 2016)

"What Shall We Do Now that the Museums Are Closed and Paris Is Blue?" *Parcel Magazine* (Summer 2015)

"Dragon" *Word Riot* (February 2015)

"Family Games" *Sixfold* (Summer 2016)

"How to Fall Out" *Atticus Review* The Lost and Found Issue (March 1, 2016)

"Chin Chin Chin" *Gravel* (April 2016)

"Sorried" *Crack the Spine* Issue 171 (November 2015); republished in *Crack the Spine* XIV (2016)

"Pop Goes the Weasel" *Moon City Review* (2017)

"Inside the Box" *Literary Orphans* Issue 26 (September 2016)

"Watch Yourself" *Oakland Review* Volume 4 (January 2017)

"Subject: Lay Off the Lays" *New South* (May 15, 2017)

"Perne in a Gyre" *Broad!* (Summer 2016)

"Squirrel Beach" *Cleaver Magazine* Issue 14 (June 2016)

"This Much" *Arroyo Literary Review* Volume 7 (Spring 2015)

CONTENTS

☾

For my sisters,
Margot Magowan and
Hilary Magowan, with love

UNDOING

WHEN IN ROME

Reasons to do it:

To get you out of my system. Because the reality of you can never match the fantasy—no matter how great you are, how skillful, how tender your touch, how inventive your sweet talk. So possessing you will take away your power. That's why I need to see your body: naked, real, unglorious. So I won't want it. Cure by poison.

Or, *carpe diem*, et cetera. Life is short, right? In two years I turn forty. Soon my life will be too unwieldy to fling (like an anarchist in a cartoon, throwing a dynamite stick) into the fire.

Grist for the mill. I need to think of you as a research project: This is a collection of information, like leaves on a nature walk, like specimens from the moon. I will observe you closely: the hair on your shins, the texture of your armpits, the color of your tongue, the way your eyes look when you come (opaque?). The feeling of your hands on my body (heavy? gentle?).

We are still strange to each other. I don't know every sock in your drawer, every bristle of your Sonicare. Likewise, you haven't known me since I was twenty-six: every bad haircut, every time I've yelled at a child or forgotten the name of a world leader or pretended to have read that book. With you, I can be new.

You remind me of the first boy I wanted, in high school. Right before summer break, I slow-danced with him on the grass. His lips, so dry, grazed my neck. Something about you—the blank squares of your glasses, the way you transfix me (because I can't have you)—makes me think of him, my first crush.

Because you don't think I will. So there is something underhanded about your flirting. You're careful—the craftsman of the double meaning, the sly line. You expect me to reject you. I should call your bluff.

☾

In a borrowed car, we drove to the waterfront to watch people fishing. We drove to get away from your apartment, which could only lead to trouble. You had your left hand on the steering wheel. I had your right hand, a new and temporary possession. I was captivated by your hand, completely preoccupied with it: I turned it over, inserted my fingers between yours, traced the fleshy part of your palm, near the thumb, examined the nicks of your wrist.

"You have such small wrists."

You turned and smiled at me. Your glasses glinted. You squeezed my hand.

When you had picked me up at the train station, I sat close to you on the seat. This hand I was examining so carefully would brush my leg now and then, as if by accident. Our eyes met and flicked away, like light touches. But we hadn't touched yet, except for that greeting hug in the station. Too long a hug, you said later that morning: "That's when I knew."

But what did you know? And why are you so much better at reading me than I am at reading you, or myself? After all,

I am a translator, a professional reader. Why are you a code I can't interpret? Like an Arabic book I once found in the library, composed of beautiful and inscrutable letters.

☾

I never undressed you. You never undressed me. As if clothes were a metaphor for the other things that came between us: my husband, your wife, all the obvious obstructions. When you unhooked my bra (you were strangely clumsy, I arched my back to help you, we both laughed as you struggled with the curved wire teeth), my sweater stayed on. I remember thinking that given the circumstances, the clothes seemed almost comically excessive: Lying on top of me, you were still wearing your shoes, your glasses.

Time, like clothes, was something you used to keep us in check: only this much, and no more. The first time you kissed me, you broke away to say, "It's ten-forty now. At eleven, we're getting up and going out to breakfast." Though it took us longer than that, because when I came out of your bathroom, bra rehooked, sweater smoothed, my face wet from splashing water on it, we stood with our foreheads pressing together, we kissed, and you temporarily turned off your meter.

I never undressed you, and lying on slatted lawn chairs sunbathing was a subtle form of torture. This was as naked as we could be together: me in a bikini, you in old, mauve bathing trunks with water-stained shorts. From hooded eyelids I studied your body, committed it to memory: sunburnt legs, bony knees, the moles on your back. Sometimes you used my distraction to advantage. Playing chicken fight in the swimming pool, both of us with a wet child on our shoulders, we tried to knock each other into the water. I grabbed your hips for leverage, and became suddenly conscious of the bunchy fabric in my hands, your cool skin. You hooked my leg, and I lost my balance and fell.

☾

When I've most wanted to hurt you back: sitting rigidly in the car outside the train station, listening to you say, "I hope what happened today doesn't mean that you'll start fooling around. It gets easier after the first time."

Or, and this is stranger, when you told me I should help Ian clean the grill. Why did that make my face feel actually hot with anger, so even the pool water couldn't cool it? Perhaps because it seemed indicative of your moral superiority: You are better than me, more thoughtful, less selfish.

But most of all, it is your silence: the way you check out, for days or weeks, the way you become not just cold but entirely vacant, an empty chair. I wish I could turn from you with such ease.

☾

"Why?" you asked me.

Sometimes you represent yourself as someone who has traveled down this yellow brick road to infidelity and has warnings to offer about the potholes. But you also imply that your own fooling around, while nothing you're proud of (you emphasize *proud*), has been understandable.

"Abstemious" is a word you apply to Diane. "She keeps her appetites in check."

I've witnessed that myself: Before anything sparked between us, when I was thinking of you two as potential friends, we had you over for dinner. When I called to invite you I asked her, as I always do, if there were any food issues, and she paused—perhaps it was my use of the word "issues"—before saying, "No." But she barely ate her scallops, she picked at dessert. She saw me notice and said, "It's lovely, Emily. It's just so rich." You saw me raise my eyebrows. We caught each other's eyes, and that exchanged glance might have been the first brick on our road. A conspiratorial flash: See what I put up with?

So for all your regrets, your implications that betrayal is not worth the trouble, I know you believe there is something understandable about cheating on a woman who picks at scallops.

It's my being drawn to you that is, in your estimation, deviant. "Ian is such a good guy."

Good Guy. The number of times I have heard that. I have fantasized about getting Ian a T-shirt that says "Good Guy," like those "Number One Dad" shirts at Target.

Well, I love Ian, and I have for twelve years. I won't dispute the title.

But I would like to show you, just once, his collection of snow globes. They line the third bookshelf of our home office, eight of them. The first one, the start of this collection, was given to him by his high school girlfriend Julie. I don't know what it commemorates; Ian is evasive when I ask. The scene inside is a glass greenhouse, and through the plastic panes (not real glass of course) you can see a tiny, scratchy tree. Red blossoms bloom there, small as sequins: a begonia, perhaps, or a camellia. On the green plastic base, written with one of those liquid silver pens (I had one myself in middle school, for using on black paper), is, "To Eye, from Jay." Their nicknames for each other.

This ex-girlfriend is still around. We see her four or five times a year: Julie Howe, Julie Crockett, now Julie Azzopardi. Two months ago we went to her wedding—the second of her weddings that I've been to. It seemed strange to make a second wedding such a production. Her dress wasn't white, but such a pale blue that from any distance it looked white. That seemed strange, too.

She came to my wedding, of course. I remember her gift: an apple-red ceramic bowl. Sometimes I serve pasta in it. Back then, eleven years ago, Ian still occasionally called her Jay, though I never heard her call him Eye.

What does collecting snow globes say about a man? That's the question I want to ask you. Or that his collection began because his ex-girlfriend, from when he was sixteen, gave him this particular one of some greenhouse, and wrote on the bottom in silver ink? What does it say about Ian that he does not select his own fetish objects? I've collected things, too—sand dollars when I was a kid, egg cups more recently—but those items meant something to me. I chose them myself.

A day or two after Julie's wedding, I looked through the open door in the office and saw Ian holding a snow globe in the palm of his hand. Of course, I knew which one it was.

More than once, I have wanted to smash those snow globes, or perhaps just that one, partly to understand the nature of the liquid inside. Not water, I don't think: something more viscous, more gelatinous. And I would like, perhaps, to pry those "glass" walls off the conservatory; I'd like to determine what tree is protected inside it.

Yes, I would like to show you the snow globes. They seem at least as relevant, as motivating, as refusing scallops. They seem to shed light on one's character. What kind of person is attracted to sealed domes? The half-circle, not even whole, not a globe after all, that sits in one's palm? Who would display them in a perfect row?

"But Emily," you might respond, "Their whole function is to be shaken." To unsettle them, to stir and disturb those sparks of snow.

☾

"Patience is a virtue," you said to me, and I am reminded of the Latin root of patience, *pati*, a verb that appears only in passive voice, that means to suffer, to endure. Passion has the same root: think of the Passion of Christ on his cross. Yet what can be more opposed to passion than patience? The gnawing of one, the tamping down of the other.

You claim that what has kept us out of bed is logistics, and the word buried in there, logic, speaks to a gap between you and me. You are rational when I am hopeless. You evoke scenarios in the future, somedays, someafternoons, when we're in the same place, and time doesn't have to be meticulously tracked. But to me those moments are irretrievably lost in the past, or belong in some parallel universe, both of us teenagers, unattached, unmoored, where there is space to be with you.

☾

You and I never had sex, though we sat on a low wall across the street from a hotel for half an hour and discussed why we shouldn't go in. You described four possible doors that hotel would lead to, which I picture as sets in a game show, tatty velvet curtains suspended from brass rods. Through Door A, we would sleep together and finally get over each other, the frenzy dissolved, the residual secret smile exchanged twenty years later. Door B was the literal anti-climax, an awkward roll in the hay that would divide us between disappointment and relief. At Door C, the worst one, we would get caught and wreck each other's lives. And Door D was the hardest to imagine: we would somehow walk off with each other, intact. That conversation ended rancorously. I got up, unsteady, and said, "Well, let's leave, then, but let's also stop pretending this is ever going to happen."

But in that alternate reality, I will carve a space for us.

We are in Rome. Why Rome? Because it is not the place where either of us live, places associated with the fundamental accessories of our lives (Ian, Diane, my children). Perhaps, in the kind of eternal return of dreams and stories, because Rome is where I lost my virginity, and I will undo that night (cheap wine, tears, brown stains of crushed mosquitoes on the walls) by replacing it with you. So, we are in Rome. You stand in front of me. Your arms are at your sides, or perhaps you lightly press my shoulders, and you look at me. But I do not meet your eyes. I am concentrating on undoing, one by one, the mock mother-of-pearl buttons of your shirt, to touch your invisible and secret skin.

WHY WE ARE WITH
THE MEN WE ARE WITH

Two drinks in, we're complaining. Jem wants a second baby, "But who the hell will gestate it?" Her husband Pete is a stay-at-home dad. I'm regretting ordering my Gibson. The cocktail onion reminds me of a bobbing eyeball: slimy and shiny, striated like bark. I poke it with my swizzle stick, envying Jem's drink, made with blood oranges, perfect like Jem.

"So why are you with him?" says Shelley.

"Oh, why the fuck are we with any of them?" says Jem. Her British accent makes even fuck lovely—*fock*—a creamy dollop dropped from a spoon. "I spend all day as this walking, talking brain in a suit. Then I come home, and Pete is stirring stew while the baby holds his leg. I just wish he made money. I don't mean a fortune—any money at all! And all we talk about is Charlotte." She looks at me now; Jem and I have been friends since freshman year in college. "You remember: I used to have intense, intellectual boyfriends. Quirky assholes, but they could talk. How did I end up marrying someone who has no conversation? Well, there's the sex, of course."

Shelley nods. We know all about their sex life. Five years in, they still do it three times a week. Every so often, Jem will let something drop: Pete blindfolded her with her mother's Pucci scarf. Or she'll apologize for being sleepy or distracted: "We were up half the night, fucking." *Focking.*

Shelley doesn't need to say why she's with Al. If a man leers at her, she gets pregnant. She and Al weren't even serious when she got pregnant with Frances, and decided she couldn't cope with another abortion. I remember four years ago, at Shelley's wedding, looking at her belly, and imagining an iron ball inside, anchoring her. Shelley used to be a hummingbird, quick and graceful. Now she sags. Not that this stops her and Jem from asking me, whenever we get together, "So when are you going to have one?"

And why am I with Michael?

Fifteen years ago, when I was a freshman at UT, he broke my heart. Jem and I met him at a kegger, but Michael focused on me, rather than the sexy English girl. After two months, he called it off. He wasn't ready to be serious. So when we bumped into each other ten years later in San Francisco, I was on a quest. Who cared about his crazy chef hours, or that he did blow or was selfish in bed?

And further back, because such over-compensation for rejection comes from somewhere old and deep: When my parents divorced, Mom took my brother Bradley, but not me. She said it would be good for the kids to live with parents of the opposite gender, for each of us to have one-on-one time with a parent who focused on just us. Besides, her new place was a two-bedroom, and Bradley and I fought nonstop.

Michael sutured old sores: that eighteen-year-old who cried in her dorm for days, listening to the Smiths; that twelve-year-old looking at the directions on a package of frozen meatballs, while her father watched football.

Before all those rejections weighed me down, became their own ingested anchors, wasn't I a hummingbird myself?

On family road trips when I was a kid, before the divorce, we'd drive by woods, and I fantasized about running away when we stopped for gas. Losing myself in those trees, climbing up and up ladderlike branches.

I watch Jem sip her radiant drink. I think of four years ago, before she had Charlotte, when she and Pete were on a break, because Jem used to do that all the time: decide he wasn't sharp enough for her. I was living with Michael by then, but he was away on a chef thing—some intensive sauce weekend in Napa. I ran into Pete in Dolores Park. We drank beers from his cooler; then we went back to his place. His sheets were unwashed. He tied my wrists to the headboard with a pair of socks. When I closed my eyes, I saw Rorschach blots in reverse: red-orange on a black background.

I listen to my two best friends talk about their men and their kids and remember looking out the car window when I was a kid, longing for those woods. I imagine standing in front of our house, holding my key, rubbing my thumb on the grooves. Then not unlocking the door at all. Putting the key under the mat. Or, better, sticking it through the mail slot so I can't have second thoughts. Hearing the ping as it hits the floor: then turning my back and taking off.

ELEANOR OF AQUITAINE

Ever since her parents split up and her father moved into his own place, he tells Ellie bedtime stories—not ones from books, but stories about her. "This is between you and me," her father says, though Ellie suspects he wants her to carry these tales back home, that the stories are spiked iron balls to catapult over her mother's fortress walls.

For instance, the one about her name. Ellie has always heard a particular narrative: She was named after the sensible sister in a novel by Jane Austen that her mother loves. But this, Mark Rosenblatt now maintains, is false.

"Your birth mother gave you the name Eleanor," he says. "We both loved it. Nonetheless Pauline wanted to change it. It's like she didn't want you marked in any way by your birth mother. I insisted you keep it."

Another night, he tells her why they needed to adopt. "Your mother had endometriosis. The thing to know about endometriosis, Ellie, is that it's painful, sure, but in no way does it compromise a woman's fertility. Pauline was not sterile, is my point. That is, until she decided she couldn't deal with the discomfort anymore and chose to get her uterus removed."

From the way her father emphasizes the word *chose*, and the way he uses *discomfort* rather than pain, as if her mother had a headache or a rash, Ellie understands the point. When

Ellie was little, her father used to ask after reading her a book, "So what's the meaning of this story?" Ellie chose her words carefully, knowing there was a right answer. The meaning of this particular story is clear: Ellie was adopted because her mother couldn't take the trouble to conceive her own child.

Hearing this makes Ellie feel sorry for her mother, whom these days she mostly hates. Ellie knows the way her father disparages pain.

His brief stint as the parent soccer coach, when Ellie was nine, was a disaster. He drove her teammates to tears with his demands that they stop being wimps, and worse. Ellie remembers the shuddery thrill of hearing an adult say "pussies."

Even now, her father rolls his eyes when Ellie begs off their hike in Tilden Park because of cramps (her period started last year).

Ellie's mother is sweet about her cramps. She mixes lemonade with sparkling water, stirring in a spoonful of raspberry jam. Together they watch old movies in which the actresses have eyebrows that look drawn with Magic Marker. Her mother says, "Poor baby. I had the worst time with cramps."

☾

Ellie's best friend Laurel wants to sleep over when Ellie is staying at her father's. Laurel loves the crazy shit he says.

Laurel's parents split up a year before Ellie's. Ellie considers Laurel's family her practice divorce, the way she hears childless adults talk about their nieces, nephews, and dogs as "practice babies." Laurel's mother is a combination of Ellie's parents: depressed and nutty like Ellie's father, distracted like her mother. Laurel's father is simply gone, vanished into the turtle shell of his new life in Portland, Oregon, with his new wife and baby.

When Laurel sleeps over at Ellie's father's house, they have to share a twin bed with flannel sheets that are too hot. Plus his apartment smells. Not bad, exactly, but funny: like dim sum that's been left out.

Ellie's father doesn't hide things parents are supposed to hide. When the weed delivery person rings the doorbell to hand him his vacuum-sealed bags of pot, or gummy edibles, he opens the door right in front of Ellie and Laurel, eating Kung Pao chicken on the couch.

He tells them that pot is better for them than alcohol. No one has ever died from pot.

He tells them boys just want pussy. Laurel laughs in delight, but Ellie remembers her father the soccer coach, freaking out her teammates and enraging their parents.

He tells them that nothing is so dangerous in this world as love. "If there's one piece of advice I have for you girls," he says, drawling as he does when stoned, "it's to avoid giving your heart to someone. Because believe me, they will crap all over it."

That night, squished in Ellie's bed, Laurel keeps giggling over that image of a heart, pulpy and red, that someone has defecated upon. "Like a shit heart instead of a chocolate heart," Laurel says.

They are stoned themselves. After Ellie's father went to sleep, they shared one of his edibles. A sugary square, it reminds Ellie of the *pates de fruits* her mother brings home in pale, rectangular boxes from her business trips to France.

"At least your Dad talks to you," says Laurel, who calls her father "emoji dad," because the typical response she gets to her emails is a smiley face, or a winking face.

Ellie listens to her father, but she does not disclose.

She doesn't tell him about her boyfriend Miles, the mere fact of him, much less that last week she let Miles take off her bra.

She doesn't tell him how her mother hums, dusting powdered sugar on Ellie's waffles.

She doesn't tell him that when her mother came out of the shower the other day, Ellie saw that she had waxed off most of her pubic hair. Now it is an arrowhead instead of a triangle.

Ellie doesn't tell him she sits on her mother's bed watching Pauline get ready for a date. Her mother asks, "Which pair, Kitten?" She holds up to her earlobes one chandelier earring, one pearl stud, and Ellie chooses.

☾

Her father suggests that Ellie pick Eleanor of Aquitaine for her eighth grade biography project. "She's your namesake," he says. When they are checking out books, he says, "Though who knows what your birth mother had in mind when she named you. I wish we'd met her. I would have asked. Maybe she was thinking about Eleanor Roosevelt? She was just a kid."

He speaks loudly, even though they are in the library. Her father doesn't modulate his voice for venues. People hush him in movie theaters, when in the middle of a film he asks Ellie what she wants for dinner.

Normally Ellie would pretend not to hear him. But information about her birth mother is so novel that she says,

"How old was she?"

"Your birth mother? Eighteen. We never met her, but she left a picture. Half Puerto Rican, half German. She had beautiful, long eyelashes. Like spider legs."

"We have a picture of her?" Ellie's voice is a high squeak.

"Your mother does. See, this I will never understand, why Pauline didn't give it to you. Why she's so threatened by your birth mother. I pointed out she had amazing eyelashes, and you should have seen Pauline's face."

What is the meaning of this story?

Later, working on her biography, Ellie wonders if her father had other reasons for suggesting Eleanor. The Duchess of Aquitaine, Eleanor became the Queen of France but was clever enough to stipulate that her property would stay her own. When she had her marriage annulled, she took Aquitaine with her. Weeks later she married Henry Plantagenet, who would become King Henry II of England. He was nine years younger.

"Shit, Eleanor of Aquitaine was a cougar!" says Laurel, delighted.

Then Ellie has to tell her the sad part: how after they had eight children, Henry fell in love with someone else, and after Eleanor helped their sons revolt against him, he locked her up. Eleanor was only released from prison when Henry died thirteen years later.

☾

Usually Ellie watches old movies with her mother. Afterwards Pauline will marcelle Ellie's hair, or make it wave over one eye like Veronica Lake's. But because this biography was her father's idea, Ellie asks him to rent *The*

Lion in Winter, about the fighting Plantagenets spending Christmas together.

After ten minutes her father goes to the kitchen and comes back, unwrapping one of his edibles. It's a light brown, sugary square, the kind that Ellie and Laurel once ate. "Want half?" he asks her.

It's hard to chew, with him watching her.

Once stoned, he enjoys the movie, slapping his knee when King Henry rushes through his castle courtyard and kicks aside a chicken. He acts like *The Lion in Winter* is a comedy. But Ellie hates how the king and queen keep attacking each other through their sons. She hides behind her hair so her father won't see her face.

☾

"What the fuck, Mark?"

Her mother's voice on the hall extension is so loud that Ellie hears her, even though Ellie is in her bedroom with the door closed. She stares at her closet floor, where her shoes line in color-coordinated rows. At her father's, they are in a heap. She is so tired she thinks she could sleep for days, in this room that smells like lavender sachets and fabric softener, not old take-out.

"What were you thinking, telling Ellie about that photo?"

Or better yet, as soon as her mother gets off the phone, she'll call Laurel. Ellie feels an urge to do something they haven't done in years: to play with Laurel's white Victorian dollhouse. Ellie is sick of being young Prince Henry or Richard the Lionheart, drafted by their angry mother into insurrections. She is sick of edibles, of studying her pubic hair in the mirror. She wants to arrange all the tiny plates and cutlery for dinner, to place the ceramic pot of stew on the tiny silver serving tray, and to sit the doll family in their chairs, napkins pleated in their laps, ready to eat.

WARMER, COLDER

Ellie started babysitting the same time I did, because that's how she gets some of her pot. After the kids go to bed, or while they watch TV, Ellie searches shelves, cabinets, the refrigerator. Once she found a baggie inside a Russian nesting doll. Even if the parents suspect her, she says, they won't accuse her. No one wants to say the word "pot" to a thirteen-year-old.

I search for other things when I'm at Mr. D's. I look through Mrs. DiPresso's bureau drawers, examine her fancy, lacy underwear. I hold her perfumes to my nose. I have two favorites, one for how it smells, like almond curd, and one for its purple, crystal bottle. Mom had an amethyst ring that Dad gave her when she turned thirty. She used to wear it every day, but after he left she put it away. I don't know where it is, or if it still is: I heard her tell Aunt Jane that she threw a bracelet he gave her into the bay. Mrs. DiPresso's perfume bottle is the same smoky purple.

Once Sadie caught me snooping, and asked what I was doing. So I turned it into a game: Warmer, Colder. I told her to think of something, anything, and I would look for it. When I got closer she should say "Warmer."

She said, "Oh, I know that Hot game."

Now we play it all over the house, though Sadie's favorite place is the pantry. I pick hard-to-see treasures: vanilla extract, a can of macadamia nuts, sprinkles for shaking onto cookies. Mrs. DiPresso keeps her pastas in big glass jars, a different jar for every noodle shape. I tell Sadie their Italian names: *farfalle* for bowties, *orecchiette* for little ears.

Before Nina was my stepmother, she took me to a fancy delicatessen where they made pasta by hand, and she taught me the names for all the shapes. Nina said everything sounds sexier in Italian. I remember the warm rumble of her whisper, her plum-colored lipstick.

Before she was my stepmother, Nina sent care packages of candy to me at summer camp. Each candy came in its own clear plastic box. She likes containers, just like Mrs. DiPresso. The boxes were so pretty I didn't want to open them, even to eat my favorite candy, Swedish fish. Those stuck to the roof of my mouth in a gummy paste.

Nina was interested in me, then.

Mom said she was just buttering me up. I remember laughing when she said that, because Mom was literally buttering one side of a loaf of bread to make garlic bread. First she mashed the garlic in butter with her pestle. That was a present from my father, too, but unlike the ring, not a gift Mom needed to hide or to destroy. Mom raised her eyebrows, like I was being rude.

"Look what you're doing," I said. Mom could still laugh at herself then.

☽

This is how it started with Mr. D.

Mrs. DiPresso was in Napa, photographing a wedding. I was babysitting Sadie so Mr. D could get some writing done. But he wasn't writing. He leaned in the doorjamb, watching

Sadie and me make spirographs. Some of the plastic shapes in the set were circles, some were footballs; they had coils of holes. I inserted the tip of the pen through a hole, and then I'd hold the pen in place while Sadie rotated the shape inside the wheel. Only six, Sadie is a perfectionist. When the spirograph wasn't a flawless star or a flower, she wanted to throw it away. We recycled a whole pile of discards.

"It's so damn hot. Let's cool off in the wading pool," said Mr. D.

While he filled the pool with the hose, I helped Sadie into her suit, red with white polka-dots. Seeing Minnie Mouse stretch over her round tummy reminded me of when my parents took me to Disneyland. Dad pretended to be a vampire feasting on Mom's neck, Mom couldn't stop laughing, and her amethyst ring burned on her finger.

The water was so cold. I sat on the plastic rim and studied my feet, bony and blue-white on the slick bottom.

Mr. D said, "Laurel, you should get in. This feels wonderful."

"I don't have a bathing suit."

"Borrow one of Bethany's."

Of course I knew that Mrs. DiPresso's bathing suits would never fit. She has hips; she is 34-D. All her bras, sheer or lacy, had bands of underwire. But I tried one on just to confirm. I looked ridiculous, a little girl in my mother's clothes. Or Nina's. I remember trying on one of Nina's sundresses once, Minnie Mouse red. Nina said, "That isn't your color."

It would be different if Mrs. DiPresso actually had a one-piece, but her bathing suits were all bikinis, meant for posing.

So I went back outside, and said nothing fit.

Mr. D said, "Well, how about you just wear your underwear."

I turned my back to take off my clothes. I was wearing my favorite shirt, the one with the lime slices. (The first time he saw it, Mr. D said, "Looking at you makes me want a margarita"). My fingers felt fat and clumsy, undoing my buttons. My shorts were easier, one snap.

We pretended this was normal, the three of us sitting in eighteen inches of cold water, me in my light pink cotton bra and underwear. Sadie splashed me. When I looked down I could see my nipples.

Afterwards Mr. D said "Laurel, you dry off," and took Sadie upstairs for her nap. That was usually my job, but not today. I lay on the grass. My skin was cold and bumpy like chicken skin, and my brain felt cold, too, not functioning properly. The sun was bright above my closed eyelids. I pictured the wet curl of Mr. D's armpit hair, like the toe of a Turkish slipper.

(Dad once got me a pair of beautiful slippers, when he and Nina went to Marrakesh: they were peacock blue, embroidered with seed pearls).

I felt Mr. D's shadow over me; his foot bumped my thigh. "Sadie's sleeping like a baby," he whispered. *Farfalle, orecchiette.* I kept my eyes closed, and after a minute I felt his hand on my belly. I stayed Snow White still, and his fingers slipped inside my still damp underwear.

There's a high fence around their yard. No neighbors can see into it. But what if Sadie had woken up? Had looked out her window? She would have seen Mr. D easing down my underwear, spreading my legs, his head dipping between them.

For a whole month we didn't do it. He said I wasn't even in high school yet. He said it was one thing to go down on me. That felt good, didn't it? Sex was serious.

But what part of me was I saving?

The third time we fooled around he stuck three fingers inside me and said, "This is what it will feel like. How does that feel, Laurel?" as he moved his fingers. I didn't like to talk, when he was touching me. I'd close my eyes and listen.

The fourth time he put the tip of his cock in me—Just the tip, he said. This doesn't count.

In July Mrs. DiPresso was off on another photo shoot, and Sadie was napping. We did it on their bed; he pulled out and came on my stomach. None of my friends have had sex, though Ellie has a boyfriend, Miles. So no one warned me the way come looked, like egg white. Nina and I painted egg white with a brush on top of her pie crust, after she and Dad got married but before she got pregnant with Jonah, before they pretty much forgot about me.

The problem with condoms is Mr. D couldn't feel anything, he said. "You should get on the pill. Except that could mean doctors, and parents, and no one can ever know about this, understand Laurel? Are you listening to me, Laurel? Maybe if you go to Planned Parenthood …."

Even though I was old enough to babysit, when Mom went out of town she'd hire Isabel Kopensky to watch me. I'd complain, "Mom, you're infantilizing me." But I liked Isabel, with her striped glasses and mermaid hair. She talked to me like I was her age, twenty ("infantilize" was her word).

She was the person I was most tempted to tell.

One time Isabel was working on an essay and I saw this phrase: "sexual harassment, broadly defined." There was a whole list of things men did to women that they wouldn't call harassment but should regard as such. On her list was, "Complain about being unable to feel sensation when using condoms." I wanted to ask her about that claim: was it fair to call it harassment? Weren't you supposed to be honest with someone you really liked?

Instead I asked her about another item on her list. "What's so bad about a man asking you to smile?"

"Because women aren't there to be pleasant and decorative, Laurel. You're allowed to frown without being fucking chastised!" she said, and then, "Sorry, excuse my language."

The thing I wanted to talk to her about was one time when Mr. D licked me, and I felt my body come apart like I was a broken doll, limbs sprung from the sockets. I said, "Oh, Jack," and he moved up so his mouth was next to my ear and whispered, "Call me Mr. D."

☾

The first three letters of Sadie's name spell "sad." I want to protect her from things: from her father falling in love with some woman with plum lipstick who can trill, liltingly, her R's.

When I was little, just before my birthday, my mother would say, "I am going to freeze you so you stay six forever!" And I'd say No, no, I want my presents, I want my ice cream cake, I want to get big. I loved that Mom wanted to freeze me but couldn't stop me from growing.

Now I want to freeze Sadie.

I want to keep her from having parents whose thin skin of the inside of their arm is cross-hatched with what looks like a Tic-Tac-Toe grid. (I said, "How did you do that, Mom?" Her eyes were dull like she couldn't see me, like I wasn't there).

At the end of the summer Sadie and Mr. D and I were sitting in their scratchy backyard, and something bit the rim of my left ear: a spider I think. My ear turned red and swelled. The cartilage didn't feel like cartilage anymore, or my skin like skin. Hot, rubbery, it felt like another material altogether: a lily pad, or a strip of tire.

Mr. D looked for calamine lotion but couldn't find any. Even though I knew where it was (in the nightstand drawer on Mrs. DiPresso's side of the bed, with something purple and shiny that I looked up on the Internet and learned is a cockring), I couldn't tell him, because then he'd know I went through their things.

So I let him anoint my ear with something else instead. I recognized it: the gel he used on me the weekend before because, "What's the matter, Laurel; why aren't you wet?"

I sat in the sun touching my ear, waiting for the poison to run its course.

BUKO

Honey, I know you think I'm the worst thing that ever happened to you. I know you tell your girlfriends all kinds of shit, and your mother won't say my name. But before we go too far down this path of restraining orders, and your pinhead lawyer, and my sad, lumpy lawyer with the wide hips who always shoves his hands in his pockets like the saddest sack who ever waddled into a courtroom: remember buko?

Buko, that baby coconut ice cream they have at Mitchell's? You got to remember that.

It was, what, our second date? But our first real date.

(The first one at that bar, El Rio, was sloppy. You nervous, drinking more than you meant to; me drinking, too. We made out in the alley by the garbage cans: your mouth was warm and wet. But then you acted like I'd taken advantage of you, instead of accepting what was offered. Not even that; I didn't take you to bed, didn't try to. I just felt your tits in that alley that smelled like coffee grounds, and chicken skin, and salad dressing, and like sweat, yours and mine, mixing.)

So: Mitchell's was our first real, official date.

You showed up, remember, honey, rigid as a ruler. You were trying to set the record straight after those alleyway kisses; you didn't want me to think you were That Girl.

So I explained about Mitchell's. "This here's a San Francisco institution!" I blared, like the guide on a tour bus. "It's been around since before my mother was born. Her older sister Adela was in my grandma's belly. All my grandma wanted to eat was ice cream, and the only flavor she wanted was buko: baby coconut. So she took my uncle Richie to Mitchell's every day and got him a sugar cone. He'd pick different flavors, vanilla, mint, *dulce de leche*, but Grandma always got the buko." I told you, "Girl, try this buko. And the right way: in a waffle cone, with that dark chocolate shell that hardens as soon as they drizzle it on. I don't know what that dark magic is, but you got to try it."

You said, "I don't like coconut."

We sat on someone's front steps. You crunched through that chocolate shell with your small, white teeth. All you could say was "Ah!" Because it's that fucking good, the buko.

(Later I would hear you make the same sound, that sigh-whisper, "Ah," when I thrust into you for the first time.)

Honey, do you remember, seven years ago, licking that chocolate shell? It was like my heart was encased in chocolate magic shell, and you bit into it.

Here's what I want to tell you.

Recriminations fly like crazy birds. They have a path of their own. You say shit, I say shit. You know those cartoons where the characters are in a lifeboat, starving, and they look at each other and hallucinate that their feathered best buddy is a fat, roasted, golden-brown chicken?

Well, there are times I believe you looked at me and saw a green card, a baby girl with hazel eyes, a rent-controlled apartment in the Mission.

There are women, believe me, who would think it's romantic for a guy to stand outside her place at night, all night, after she kicked him out. Didn't you see *Say Anything*, girl? I'm no stalker.

Which is not to discount that I scared you, or that you felt threatened, and belittled, and degraded. All of your big, big words.

Scratch that, I didn't mean it.

All I am trying to say, honey, is this: Don't you remember? Sitting on those warm, sun-soaked, concrete steps? You in your soft, old blue jeans, threading apart at the knee, your knee almost touching mine? Between those white, frayed, cotton threads, cornsilk covering the ear, your golden skin? You biting, with small, sharp teeth, into that buko?

I introduced you to that. Honey, that was me.

BRINING

For years, people had told Ben and Miriam to try brining their turkey: That was the sure fix for the typical glitches of Thanksgiving, the dried-out problem, the over-cooked problem. Ben was skeptical. Turkey, in his estimation, was a serviceable food when deployed properly—say, sliced, within a sandwich—but would disappoint when forced center stage.

In their couple, Miriam took on the role of the convention-subverter; she was the one who lobbied for Pakistan versus London for a family trip. But she refused to meddle with Thanksgiving, though Ben knew Miriam found turkey just as unimpressive as he did. Left to her own devices, extricated from the influence of her brother Ethan, from her sister-in-law Lynn, whose face was as flat and round as a plate, or from her recently widowed mother, all three of whom they would be hosting, Miriam would blow off the inevitably underwhelming turkey and go for something dynamic: paella, bouillabaisse, something worth the hours of sweat. Ben was convinced of this.

As it was, though, she said, "This year, I'm going to brine it."

She looked at him, awaiting the rant. Instead, Ben volunteered to get a twenty-four-gallon plastic bucket.

Miriam's eyes sharpened, then: they became as pointy and precise as the pencils their daughter would whir into barblike condition and perfectly line up on her desk. "Thanks," she said, after taking, Ben felt, his full measurement.

"Anything else we need?"

"Wine. Beaujolais. Ethan will bring something crappy."

"Sure. Flowers?"

His question seemed to sharpen Miriam's eyes one last notch. Ben was not, and never had been, a purchaser of flowers. But she was busy: Her hands were floury with pie crust. "If you see anything pretty."

Starting the car, Ben tried to calm his racing heart. Since they were undergraduates, since he first met her, Miriam had always been smarter. Back in college, her meticulous notes in a maniac's handwriting had lifted Ben into many an A. But there were times when it would be expedient to be married to someone less sharp.

He reflected, as he had frequently in recent weeks, upon the difficulty of assessing when his behavior was suspicious.

There was too much latitude for suspicion, was the problem. Being cooperative and helpful was potentially suspicious, as was being romantic. But so was being brusque, distracted, critical, or cranky. He felt like he was navigating some tricky video game, quicksand everywhere; then he questioned why this mental picture dressed itself as a video game, instead of some real (if still imaginary) bayou. Was Ben that severed from reality these days, that his fantasies packaged themselves in pixels?

Something needed to change.

He went to Target first, to get the errand out of the way. There was no predicting the lines the day before Thanksgiving, except that they would worsen as the afternoon unrolled. He congratulated himself for choosing Target, relatively empty, rather than packed-to-the-rafters

Whole Foods. The problem was the limited options for wine and flowers, but Ben persuaded himself that a cellophane arrangement of red leaves and brass chrysanthemums was seasonal, and that the flowers would hold up in his car for an hour.

An hour was all he had time for; an hour, with Thanksgiving press, was plausible. He wasn't willing, when he considered Miriam's pencil-point eyes, to risk more.

He parked down the block from Annie's house. He put the flowers on the car floor, along with three bottles of Beaujolais, and tucked the fourth under his arm.

Annie's front yard was overgrown, strewn with leaves.

The day before, he had filled two Hefty bags with his own yard's leaves, thinking, as he scooped them up in crackly handfuls, of when he had picked up Miriam at the salon the week before to save her the walk home. Her stylist unsnapped a silver plastic shawl from Miriam's neck; all around her swivel chair were trimmings of Miriam's hair.

"How sweet of you to pick her up." The stylist, improbably named Lisbon, beamed at him. Miriam's eyes, though pleased, were appraising.

Annie's yard was a mess. Her leaves reminded him less of hair clippings than of the debris he associated with Annie: her desk overflowing with papers that he wanted to straighten and corner, bowls full of paper clips, buttons, a thimble. How intensely Ben wanted to rake her yard; it felt like a compulsion. But of course there was no time for that. He pressed his thumb on the doorbell.

Annie opened the door. "Darling," she said, and buried her nose in his sweater.

Ben waited a few seconds before lightly pushing her back into her house, and closing the door behind them.

He handed her the wine. Annie said, "I already opened some. Want a glass?"

While she poured, Ben looked at his watch: 1:58. Early for a bottle of wine to be half empty. Perhaps she had opened it the night before? Her teeth, he saw when she turned back to him, were tinged red.

"God, Ben, I've missed you."

He took a sip of wine (not good; Annie's wine was usually not good. She seemed to have no principle of selection, beyond an eye-catching label). Annie put her arms around him, knocking his hand, spilling wine onto the sleeve of Ben's sweater.

"Careful!"

"Oh, sorry. I can wash that for you. Take it off."

"I don't ...." Ben was about to say, I don't have time, but stopped. He pulled off his sweater.

"Mmm! See, that was a ploy to get you to take off your clothes." Annie turned on the kitchen tap.

"Water won't remove a wine stain. Don't you have white wine vinegar and salt?"

She stared at him. Funny how the two women in his life looked at him. Their eyes, like the rest of them, were yin-yang opposites, but both sets wounded in different ways: Miriam's pencil points, Annie's teary. She was so damn sensitive, no shell at all.

"Annie ...."

She turned her back and opened a cabinet. "Does it have to be white wine vinegar?"

"Yes, because—."

"Let me guess: it has to be Chardonnay."

This was new, this bite to Annie.

"Here you go. I don't want to misapply it somehow.

Further screw up your sweater."

Silently, Ben took the bottle of vinegar.

Annie's angry blue eyes refilled. "Sorry! I don't know what's wrong with me!"

"It's OK," said Ben. He drizzled vinegar on the spot. "Do you have salt?"

Annie handed him a carton of Morton's. Ben tipped a pinch of salt on the stain. After eyeballing the countertop (the mystery of Annie's perpetually sticky kitchen, it was as if she scrubbed her counters with syrup), Ben flattened his sweater on top. "Disaster averted."

He was trying to be light, but Annie grimaced. "Right. My house is full of booby traps."

Enough already, Ben thought. "Well, your boobs are traps."

Annie's lip, quivering, turned up. She put her arms around him and lifted her face to be kissed.

Embracing Annie, a thought pinballed in Ben's mind. He did suspect Annie of carelessness.

Not so much of consciously spilling wine, but of not caring if they were caught. She encouraged him to park in her driveway; she bugged him to take her out to dinner at the Crab Apple, where they could easily run into people they knew. Ben was starting to feel, when he left Annie, the need to examine himself for gold bobby-pins secreted in his pockets.

Ben's friend Mitchell had been caught in an affair when his girlfriend deliberately left her hairclip on the keyboard of his wife's computer. Now Mitchell was living in a grim apartment with a hissing radiator, his wife divorcing him. Mitchell was philosophical. "Well, Lisa wanted me to herself," he said. Ben remembered Mitchell's blended tone: chagrined but flattered.

It wasn't like Annie hid her hopes. They were the same as that Lisa's (Ben had never met Lisa the Mistress, but pictured her as leggy, aerobicized). The difficult thing to sort out was not what Annie wanted—she was her transparent self—but what Ben did.

Ben's desires were a bird that wouldn't stay on one branch but kept taking flight. His were desires, plural, and consequently irreconcilable, whereas Annie's desire focused on him.

Oh, he certainly wanted Annie. Not so much her boobs: Despite his "booby traps" joke, Annie's breasts were the one part of her body Ben did not find particularly attractive. Small, sagging, the skin thin and papery, the nipples disproportionately large and brown, too dark for her pale skin: Her breasts reminded Ben of tea bags. When he fantasized about Annie, he always modified her breasts, pumped them fuller, made her nipples pink and round as quarters. But her legs were extraordinary: muscular from running and as long as his. There was no sensation like the grip of Annie's legs around his back.

But he also wanted Scrabble with Miriam by their fireplace. He wanted the elated expression she got, landing the Q on the double letter, "quixotic" on the triple word. "This is," she had declared, "the greatest moment of my life!"

He wanted Miriam's taste and Annie's admiration. He wanted to suck Miriam's nipples (her breasts, even at forty-one, her best feature) and to be gripped by Annie's legs. He thought of a flipbook Edith had loved when she was little. The pages divided into thirds, so you could combine the illustrations to produce a body with a fireman's head, a ballerina's tutued torso, an astronaut's silver-booted legs.

"I'm sorry I'm so moody," Annie said, breaking the kiss. "The holidays suck. It's so unfair, that Hud gets Skylar for Thanksgiving and Christmas, too."

"Sorry." Ben tangled his fingers in Annie's bushy, pre-Raphaelite hair. *Sorry*, the epitome of an inadequate word: He tried to count how many times they had volleyed it today.

"Skylar was happy to leave because he's taking her to some stupid ice-skating rink. Hud has been a shitty father his whole life, doesn't do a single carpool, never goes to parent-teacher night. Then when we finally split up, so when it's no use to me, he decides to become this fun dad? I can't believe Skylar falls for it." Her eyes welled again.

"Sorry, honey," repeated Ben, but now he twisted his hand in her hair to see his watch. Forty-five minutes left at the outside.

"I hate Hud."

Even the name, short for Hudson, was ugly: It sounded like a bowling ball dropped on the floor.

Ben had done his commiserating time, he told himself, his fingers groping Annie's breast. He had listened to Annie's litany: Hud's total lack of interest in Skylar until Annie had finally kicked him out, or, more precisely, didn't allow him to come back the last time he left. But now Hud wanted, competitively, Annie believed, as an act of hostile one-upmanship, to lure Skylar from her mother.

Poor Annie. She was involved in more than one love triangle.

And Ben had heard about Hud's drinking, his verbal abuse, the names he called Annie: a bad cook, a slob, an overly indulgent mother, a moron. (The first three of those things Ben privately considered true.) He had heard about Hud closing his eyes when they had sex; Annie was convinced he had imagined himself with someone else.

Hud reminded him of the chapter books Edith had wanted him to read aloud before she was old enough to read to herself, that awful series in particular about the fairies. It had gotten to the point where Miriam and he would rock-paper-scissors for who had to read those damn books. Doing dishes was preferable, folding laundry was preferable, scrubbing toilets, Miriam had maintained at one point, was preferable to reading that dreadful story one more time. Kissing Annie, backwards-walking her to her unmade bed while they still had time to have sex (forty minutes now), Ben thought this may well be the true definition of love: subjecting oneself, willingly, for the sake of one's beloved, to boredom.

☾

It was 3:15 when Ben got back in his car. Despite the fact that the temperature was in the forties, he lowered his window. There had been no time to take a shower. The wine stain on his sweater was a faded but visible bruise.

As soon as he entered his house, he could smell baking pies. He carried the plastic bucket into the kitchen. Miriam stood at the counter, trimming stems from mushrooms. She looked up, meaningfully, at the kitchen clock.

"Where the hell were you?"

"The lines…" Ben said. He dropped the bucket on the floor as if it were heavy, instead of simply cumbersome. "Hang on, let me get the rest of it."

His heart raced as he gathered the wine bottles and flowers from the passenger side floor. It had been difficult to extract himself. In bed, Annie had gotten on top, as if she wanted to pin him, her long, strawberry-blond hair suffocating him. Then later, more tears about how hard it was to be alone on Thanksgiving.

If Annie were a plant, she would cling. Whereas Miriam would be full of fine needles that stung.

Ben set the wine and flowers on the counter. Miriam wrinkled her nose at the chrysanthemums. At Target, they had struck Ben as festive, the color of doorknobs, but under the kitchen lights they looked cheap and dry.

"Can I explain to you how brining works?" Miriam said. "Every single recipe says you need to leave the turkey in the salt solution for twenty-four hours."

"The lines," Ben said again, and then, again, he stopped, because Miriam closed her eyes. He looked at Miriam's fingers splayed on their countertop. She stayed perfectly still, as if giving Ben time to study her.

"Ben, allow me to give you some advice," Miriam said. "Don't say anything stupid. Better yet: don't do anything stupid." She picked up her paring knife and began, again, trimming mushrooms. "Anything else stupid."

He watched her hands, deft and efficient. Under the plastic cutting board, Miriam had inserted wet paper towels to keep it from sliding. He knew this even though he couldn't see them. He knew the precautions his wife took. Wet paper towels: the thought couldn't be more errant. Suddenly Ben felt like crying.

He picked up the ugly flowers and started unwrapping the cellophane, embossed with, he now saw, the red bull's-eye logo of Target.

"Leave them," Miriam said, without looking up.

"Let me just get them in a vase."

Perhaps because his voice cracked, Miriam nodded. She

let Ben get a vase out of the cabinet and clip the stems, puckered at the ends, without telling him to use the other vase, without directing him to cut the stems on the diagonal, without reminding him to add the envelope of revitalizing powder that Target, in any case, did not sell. Ben felt her eyes on him while he found the large coaster to put under the vase so their dining room table didn't get a watermark.

After he left the kitchen Ben went upstairs, closing the door to their home office behind him. Tomorrow this room would be inhabited by Miriam's brother and sister-in-law. The home office was directly above their kitchen. The sound-proofing in their house had always been bad, to the point that giggling Miriam held her hand over Ben's mouth when they had sex, so their daughter Edith, two doors down, wouldn't hear him.

Ben opened his email, the private new account. It had been difficult to come up with a password Miriam wouldn't guess. His wife knows him: this thought made his eyes fill. For a subject heading he typed "It's over." He pressed send. When the email program asked him if he was sure he wanted to send an email to Anne J. Sarbaines without any content, he clicked, Yes.

For the past two months Ben had considered leaving Miriam; it was only as his email winged towards its target that he understood how concretely he had pictured a life with Annie. Not just raking her impossible lawn, but planting some-thing pretty: a rhododendron bush, something that would bloom. He had been evaluating the two women, contrasting them, doing that Frankenstein-creature flipbook thing.

Only now did Ben understand that the dilemma for him was never whom he loved more: The answer to that was obvi-ous. No, the lure of Annie was her feelings for him, not his for her. To Annie, he was the competent cleaner of gutters, the passionate lover, the consistent, wise father from whom to solicit parenting advice. He loved the image of himself that she beamed back.

The revelation was as clear and sharp to Ben as a picture materializing from the smoke of a Polaroid.

Years later, Ben wishes he had been able to maintain this clarity, that he was able to follow Miriam's instruction to not do "anything else stupid."

But breakups are rarely as simple as clicking "Send without content." Fourteen days later, he replied to Annie's eighth or ninth hysterical email; he fucked her again, and then again, closing his eyes. He drove Miriam, by blatantly disregarding what was, after all, real advice, into cracking his password, which was random enough that decoding it involved installing an expensive Spy program in his computer, one that memorized keystrokes.

Three days before Christmas, Miriam hurled clothing at him, including something that hurt on impact, a belt, and shouted, "I want you to fucking leave!"

Ben was packing a suitcase, which he later realized he packed like a lunatic, throwing in three bathing suits but only one pair of underwear. He was trying to figure out where to go because he now understood, with certainty, that he would not be driving to Annie's. He turned and saw Miriam in the doorway. She might have been standing there a long time, watching him; Ben had been too busy self-imploding to sense her presence.

Miriam said, "Correction: what I really meant was, I want you to fucking stay."

She allowed him to hold her, then; she buried her face in his chest. Ben kept kissing the top of her head. They both cried. Miriam said, "We could brine a turkey in this pool of tears." She said, "Tears have the same water-to-salt ratio as a brine solution, did you know?" She said, "We need to pull ourselves together before Edith comes home."

They stayed married for another thirteen years.

At age fifty-four Miriam tells him one day she has met someone else. When Ben asks if she is in love with this other man, whose name is Lester, she says, "I wouldn't use the word 'love,' but I also wouldn't rule out its future use."

Ben, fifty-five, wonders if everything would have gone differently, if Lester would have never materialized, if Miriam would never leave, if he had only been able to hold onto that moment of perfect, sharp-edged clarity: 3:43 p.m., the day before Thanksgiving, 2002.

PALIMPSEST

A teacher of mine, known for sleeping with his students, once explained "context" like this: A man and a woman meet, go home, have sex. In the morning, she wakes. He has gone. There is this note on her pillow: "Thank you. You're amazing. I want to see you again. Please (underlined) call me," and a number to reach him. Or, second scenario: "Thank you, Sarah." (But her name is Sharon, and there is no number.) Or, there is a hundred dollar bill. The same event has happened, but what comes after defines what has taken place: She's made love, she's had a one-night stand, she's gotten screwed. Context, he told us, defines everything.

Recently, a man asked me how many lovers I've had, and I said eight. But the truth is, it depends on how you count. Do I count the ones who I decided didn't count? "It never happened."

This is something that never happened to me:

Once in college I had sex with a boy, one of my best friends. The next day, I was walking down the dormitory stairs, he was walking up. We stopped on the landing. I said, "Hi," he said, "Hi," we made it clear that nothing had happened. Twelve years later, still neither of us has mentioned that night.

Did I ever sleep with the man who asked me how many lovers I had? We agreed in the morning—in the several mornings—that we hadn't. The conspiratorial, truncated discussion: "Nothing happened, right?"

"Right."

I never started to unzip my boots and had them stick, and he never unzipped them for me. We never kissed, we never undressed each other, we certainly never made love (that one is easy). He never made me coffee in the morning, but had to pour out the first cup, because the milk had gone sour. Nothing went sour.

I could go on, but why?

Before I teach, I erase the chalkboard, and I can never tell what I am erasing: The symbols there could be math or could be Greek. All I know is I can't read them. But there is a certain relish in erasing them, and my students laugh about my energetic wiping away: "What the hell is that class?"

"Who cares? It's gone."

And I put my own marks on the board, and leave them there for someone else to erase, mark over.

Sometimes I look at the board and see the ghost writing through the legible script. I wonder, in an abstract sort of way, how many things and people I can make disappear, simply by agreeing not to read them.

ON AIR

The pictures Alice has always had of this state, and the idioms she has heard used for it, regard tunnels and holes: One is low, one is in a pit. Like the elderly lady in that LifeCall ad, one has fallen down and can't get up.

But she feels the opposite: Instead of too much gravity, anchoring her onto the Earth, there isn't enough.

Alice floats. The image in her head is of a *Curious George* book she used to read when Laurel was small, George the monkey suspended high above a New York cityscape, clutching a bouquet of balloons. (So boring, that book! Nathan refused to read it. Nathan treated parenting as a menu, from which he could choose the entertaining items.)

Far below, Alice can see her obligations: the shower stall to wash her hair, which is greasy and limp; groceries to put away; Laurel waiting for a ride to school; the portfolios Alice needs to grade. They are hundreds of feet below.

How will she reach them? By burping, like Charlie in the *Willy Wonka* film, making himself descend? But Charlie and Grandpa Joe had incentive: They didn't want to be hacked into pieces by the propeller fan at the top of the shaft. What makes the ground an appealing place for Alice?

☾

Alice used to care about things: about Laurel and Nathan, massively, but also about her art, her students, her house, potential stains on her black granite countertop. "Mom, calm down," Laurel would say, while Alice rubbed and rubbed at some smear. "It's just a—" and then stop, searching for the exact word.

Even when she was tiny, Laurel was always precise. "No, it hurts *here*," she would say to Alice, moving Alice's fingertip on her stomach half an inch to the left. Alice, precise herself (much of her artwork involves rulers and protractors) would wait, enjoying Laurel's grasp for the perfect word. Nathan was less patient.

Now, it's as if Alice's ears are packed with cotton, or as if Laurel is talking to her through whatever the aural equivalent would be to the wrong end of a telescope: some mechanism that mutes normal speech to an almost inaudible hum.

"You should go to a doctor, Mom."

What kind of doctor? Alice wants to ask. Someone who will pull the cotton out of Alice's ears, twirling it like spun sugar onto a long wand? Laurel is thinking of a shrink of course. Alice needs, Laurel recently said, to give a shit. (Odd expression, Alice thinks as she floats: who would want to be given shit?)

What Alice needs is not pills so much as gravity boots.

☾

When Nathan first started sleeping with Nina, Alice could sense it, though she didn't know what she was sensing: A shape was slowly taking form. A shape that had something to do with Nathan's sudden interest in moving to Portland; with search engine results that seemed like dots that must connect (Portland real estate, Portland radio stations, but also, more randomly, recipes for cassoulet).

Some of the clues were pure cliché: Nathan started running; the softness around his middle melted away. He bought new sweaters that were black or charcoal, tighter than the kind of slouchy and shapeless stuff he used to wear. But it was also the books he started reading in bed: Garcia Márquez suddenly, and Borges. The expression on his face was so attentive. He read with a blue pen in his hand.

Alice watched her non-reading, non-exercising, non-cooking husband mark lines and lace sneakers and soak cannellini beans overnight, and a shape took form. It was like negative space in a drawing, that blank wedge that determines the solid flesh of the bent arm, hand on hip. Or, more precisely, it was as if there were an invisible person in the room, whose body materialized when one flung towards it billows of ash, or bags of powdered sugar.

What is it? Alice thought, before she started asking, Who is it? (Filling the blank of the first question one day, as she drew charcoal along the straight edge of a ruler, Alice had thought: "Mid-life crisis." That, finally, snapped the still-bulky shape into place, gave it contours: a waistline, breasts, hips.)

☾

Alice begged Nathan to go to couples therapy, saw his capitulation as a sign that he was still willing to try, despite indicators to the contrary. (He refused to stop talking to Nina. When Alice said, "I love you," he pressed his lips together as if to keep an involuntary response from seeping out.)

But when they got there, Nathan spun therapy like a dreidel. Instead of the hour involving him consenting to that baseline first step (stop talking to Nina), he said, "We have a ten-year-old daughter, Laurel. What is the best way to tell her that I'm leaving?"

If Dr. Stuyvesant was caught off guard, he didn't show it. And so the conversation turned: "You need to tell her together. Make it clear that you both still love her; it's not her," while Alice's brain dissolved into particles.

Brain bits looped that hackneyed breakup snippet, "It's not you, it's me," sampled and twisted it—"It's not you, Laurel, it's your mother. Your distracted, flaky, never-wants-to-fuck mother," "It's not you I love, Alice, it's Nina"—until Alice wasn't sure if anybody had ever said that line to her, or if "It's not you, it's me" was just word debris, lifted from some cobwebby script that everyone had masticated with grinding, collective-consciousness teeth.

Both men looked at her expectantly: Alice blinked at them, stupefied. The only thought her smashed brain could form was, Why was I always the one who had to read *Curious George*?

That was when Alice began to float.

☾

All she wants to make is whiteness. Alice prepares her parchment with gouache, but then, instead of pulling out her charcoals and paints, layers on more gouache. Layer after layer, the white thick and shiny, starting to crackle like eggshell: not chicken but something substantial, ostrich, something that one needs a ball-peen hammer to crack. She starts to scratch it with her X-Acto blade, but then that seems wrong, just as wrong as a paintbrush or a Conté was wrong. She realizes this time the problem isn't the implement but the canvas.

The X-Acto blade on the skin of her forearm is satisfying, then throbs: She cross-hatches a grid onto her arm before she stops. Alice rinses the blade under the tap, washing away the blood, then wraps a wet paper towel around her arm. The blood keeps beading. Finally she goes to Walgreens to buy a padded bandage the size of a deck of cards.

In art school, she got a tattoo of a chameleon on her shoulder blade; it was protected by a patch like this. For Nathan, who thought tattoos were sexy, who loved to lick and nibble her shoulder, and who called Alice Karma Chameleon.

☾

Here's another thing that happened: From her floating perch, Alice makes herself regard it. When Laurel was four, and Alice thirty-two, Alice had an abortion. They had a CVS prenatal test in the tenth week. They hadn't done any genetic testing for Laurel, but Nathan's cousin recently had a baby with Down Syndrome, and that, combined with her age, made Alice want the test. Nathan had been reluctant, and when they got the results, unpersuaded. Because the results were uncertain: There was a deletion on chromosome 19, that's what the genetic counselors could tell them. But as for what it meant, they had no idea. It could be very serious: It could mean their baby would be born, for instance, without muscles. Or it could be nothing at all.

"Without muscles?" Alice repeated. She was an artist, but here was an image she couldn't picture. Did it mean skin would hang on the bone, loose and flapping, like too-big clothes?

The answer about what to do was clear to her, but inversely clear to Nathan. He had seized onto, "It could mean nothing at all" rather than "Without muscles." They wrangled for three days. In the end her choice prevailed: it was her body. But he was silent at the clinic, his hand in hers inert. Later he had to be asked four times before he fetched a heating pad for Alice to hold against her stomach.

When Laurel said, "What's the matter with Mommy?" Alice heard him say, "Mommy's..." and only after the longest pause, the kind of pause that Laurel would take, looking for the perfect word, "Sick."

Is the glass half full or half empty? Ever since, Alice has thought the better conundrum would be, "Is the fetus healthy or damaged?" The genetic counselors couldn't give them odds, couldn't give them real information at all. What was happening inside Alice's body was guesswork, hidden by its own bands of flesh and muscle.

Finally, Nathan pulled himself together. "I need you to be strong for me!" Alice said. After another long pause, he nodded. They took Laurel to the beach (the poor kid had had a tough week, Alice cramping and miserable, Nathan silent, sulking). They watched her crouch beside tide pools, poke at a starfish with a stick, touch its granular, rough body.

But was that rupture ever really repaired, that stain scrubbed away?

It was the one time Nathan cried, during that couples therapy session: when Dr. Stuyvesant asked why Laurel was an only child, and he said, "We almost had a son."

☾

"Alice, we need to talk about Laurel."

Through the invisible cotton packing in her ears, Alice hears Isabel Kopensky, the babysitter, say this. She hears her daughter's name and then, delayed, she hears her own. She snaps, "Call me Mrs. Haven."

"But you said—," Isabel bites her lip, then complies. "OK. Mrs. Haven."

Call me Alice—that is of course what Alice said, what she always tells her students; Isabel had taken her painting class before she ever started babysitting Laurel.

Alice was twenty-six when she married Nathan. Most of her friends kept their maiden names, and when Alice did take Nathan's, it was for aesthetics: "Haven" sounded prettier than "Horowitz." Under the name Alice Haven she has had seven shows, one in Chicago. She can't give it up now, any more than those famous actresses who still cart around the last name of some long-forsaken first husband. This is the story Alice tells herself.

But how does this account for her snappish insistence on "Mrs.," which she can tell from Isabel's face, almost twitching to repress a spasm, an eye roll, sounds absurd?

Alice isn't her grandmother. Grammy believed that divorced women should hold onto their ex-husband's last name until they marry again: like moving to a new horse on the carousel ride, clutching its pumping pole.

The truth is, it's something closer to spite. Alice is almost sure Nina would never have changed her name had Alice been willing to release her own hold on it. But she is entitled to it! she wants to shout at Nina Durante-Haven. It belongs to her.

So immersed is Alice in this imaginary conversation with her grandmother's nodding head, Isabel's grimacing one, Nina's outraged one, that she hears only the end of Isabel's speech.

"So I'm really worried about her."

"What?"

Again, Isabel twitches: The effort to summon up patience is so visible. It is intended, Alice thinks, to be visible. "You must notice! I know Laurel wears all those layers, it's easy to disguise, but you must see she's too thin …."

"I was a skinny girl, too," Alice says.

Isabel shakes her head. She sits at Alice's computer ("Do you mind?" she asks, though she doesn't wait to see if Alice objects). Alice watches Isabel's shiny nails click across the keyboard.

These pro-ana sites, what on earth? Alice combs through them after Isabel leaves. She reads recipes for cleanses that remind her of the days when she was confronting the negative shape of Nina, and one of the dots to connect was Nathan's interest in cooking (Tuscan food, Sardinian food; he went to the seafood store in the Mission to buy octopus).

Alice has not noticed any red thread bracelet on Laurel's wrist, but suddenly she can picture that wrist: delicate, bony. The image is a hairball coughed out of her mind.

She remembers a fairytale she used to read Laurel, about a fairy who ate only air. Alice goes to Laurel's room: The bed is neatly made. Laurel's yellow bear with the spectacles sits on her pillow, guarding it. On Laurel's bed is a green vellum book, her new journal. Alice has never touched it because (she tells herself) she respects Laurel's privacy. But the truth is it was a gift from Nina, for Laurel's recent fourteenth birthday, which makes it kryptonite.

What will she find if she opens it? This pro-ana crap? Lists of calories? Or anxieties about Alice, herself? "Mom is so fucked up …."

Avoiding it, Alice studies the bookshelf instead. It takes her a minute to find the fairytale book. There it is, the story about the fairy Rosebud who lived on air. "Like this," Alice remembers Laurel saying, opening and closing her mouth like a fish.

There's another familiar story. Hunched over the book, Alice straightens when she sees it. The story about the two sisters, one bad, one good. Every time the bad one speaks, toads and lizards hop out of her mouth; the good one, instead, utters pearls. Laurel had loved that story, too, but it horrified Alice. How awful, to have to spit out, whenever one talked, pearls! And what are pearls, anyway, but irritations: the speck of sand that the oyster protects itself from, sealing and resealing the grain to keep it from hurting the oyster's sensitive tissue.

What a thing to convert into treasure.

Alice pictures her white gouache, shiny and thick. She touches, protectively, the grid on her forearm (the scab has fallen off; it will definitely scar). If she were the good sister, the one who speaks pearls, Alice would never open her mouth again.

☾

Nathan doesn't want to be here. Every line in his body broadcasts resistance: the way he avoids contact with Alice, his rigid face. She can picture him narrating all this to Nina, how remote he was, how loyally distant.

Alice has the cotton-in-ears problem again, but she hears his distrust in the way he says the word "tactics." Spits it, really: a round, luminous pearl.

"Look at your daughter," Alice says.

She gestures: They are standing on the porch. Laurel is walking towards them, skateboard under her arm. She has not looked up yet; she doesn't yet realize her father is standing here, six hundred miles from where he lives. Alice hasn't mentioned any of it (her call, the unplanned visit from Dad), because she didn't know if she could persuade Nathan to come, or if he would trot out the same excuses: no time, so busy with the new baby.

"What—"

"Just look at her, Nathan."

While he looks at Laurel, Alice looks at him. She is descending, a long, slow fall from a precarious height. First her toes, then her heels, land on the wooden slats of the porch. She feels wobbly, as if she has sea-legs still: but under her feet there is solid ground. She watches the expressions (annoyance, perplexity, then concern) shift and slip across her ex-husband's face.

"I'm looking," he says at last.

WHEELS INSIDE WHEELS

1967

Her death is sudden, so there is no time to prepare—no protracted sickness. A stroke: Henry wakes to find her dead beside him, stiff and cool.

You have never met Elaine. You have only seen pictures: the one on his desk with the lacquered frame, and the wedding picture on the hall table that one time you went to their house, when Elaine was visiting their son in college. I imagine you encountering that picture of Elaine in her white gown and dark lipstick. You had to study it quickly; Henry's hand was on your shoulder, ready to propel you to the guest bedroom. He wouldn't have sex with you in their bed. Their bed, where a year later she dies.

So I imagine you had only seconds to absorb Elaine's face, her hair thick and glossy, a pelt. Seconds to take in the knickknacks flanking the picture: porcelain boxes with brass hinges, shaped like fruits and vegetables. You recognized the Limoges boxes because your aunt Harriet has one. Cherries on a stem, a peapod, a radish, an avocado half. You touched the bulbous pit of the avocado. "She collects them," Henry said, before steering you away.

Now, when he tells you Elaine's body was cool, you think of that porcelain avocado pit.

A stroke. She was only forty-seven, younger than Henry, though not, of course, as young as you. After he calls, you spend the whole day thinking about the word *stroke*: strokes of luck, clocks chiming, petting the silky fur of Persian cats.

Going to the funeral could be construed as respectful: the least you owe her, this woman from whom you have siphoned. But Henry emphatically does not want you there. He does not want you anywhere near there. Consider sneaking in anyway. Who is Henry to order you away? The hot way he said "No," when you said "Should I?" But you don't have the courage, finally, to defy him.

He needs time, he says, and while you could retort that you have given him plenty of time—nearly five years—instead you nod. Because he can't see you nod—you are talking on the phone—say, "I understand."

There is a joke your friend Hannah told you. Why does the adulterous man stay with his wife? Because the mistress will always understand; because the wife will never understand.

☾

When you were growing up in Kansas City and you got sick, your mother would prepare a queue of foods. First, clear broth; then, dry toast and flat ginger-ale; finally, soft-boiled eggs. Always that order, stepping-stones to recovery.

Design your own regimen. One week eat only red foods: raspberries, tomatoes, roasted beets that turn your very urine red. Think of that line in *Wuthering Heights* where Catherine Earnshaw describes her dreams going through her "like wine through water." Perhaps because your name is Catherine, you always loved that character, selfish and vicious, desired by everyone.

Do not call Henry. Instead, take long walks. For years, you have kept to your wedge of San Francisco—North Beach, Nob Hill, the Financial District—but now walk all the way to Ocean Beach. On these wanderings, talk to Henry in your head. At first, be cheerful and patient. Discuss plans to go somewhere sunny. You can swim and drink margaritas, you can help him grieve. As the weeks go by, though, and you don't hear from him, these conversations alter. They begin, "How can you."

From the shore of Stowe Lake, watch a couple peddle-boating. Think of the man before Henry: Ricky, your first lover. When you got pregnant, he offered to marry you. You were twenty, Ricky twenty-two. His expression was grim and despairing. But still, he could claim those words—"I asked you to marry me"—so deny any accountability for the back-alley abortion that left you (you were told) unable to have children. He could break up with you and have a conscience as clean as the aluminum sinks in his lab. Ricky was so skillful at blaming you for what he wanted you to do. Eight years later, you understand this is how he can love himself. But then, you were wrecked, like that doctor told you your uterus was wrecked. You moved to San Francisco in 1959 because it was the farthest you could go without sinking.

On your walks, observe San Francisco changing. It is the summer of 1967. In Golden Gate Park, see girls wearing ponchos, and they are the age you were when you moved here. Feel old and longing. From a card table on Haight Street, one girl sells tie-dye shirts. Buy a blue-and-yellow one that makes you think of wheels inside wheels.

☾

Have a drink with Hannah, who is now your only friend, because Bea had no tolerance for your relationship with a married man. Hannah tells you she saw Henry in Grace Cathedral, and that after the service, he was surrounded with women: widows, a divorcée. "Like flies to a syrup pour. Don't wait too long," she says.

He told you he needs time.

Concentrate on his defects: His teeth are stained. He is fifty-one; you are twenty-eight. But who else will want you, crooked as you are?

So test that: Convert the rhetorical question into a real one. Timid 1950s girl, you have slept with two men in your entire life: Now, have sex with another. Meet him at Vesuvio's, the bar next to your favorite bookstore; go home with him. His skin makes you think of bourbon shots. Feel tempted to stay in his Victorian flat with its view of Alcatraz, a helmet in the bay. But do not ask for his last name; do not give him your phone number.

Try LSD. Put a tab with a picture of a windowpane on your tongue: Feel you are stepping through that window into an underwater world. Drag your hand past your face and see contrails. Your hand is a dinosaur with a horned frill.

☾

Assemble on your bed all the presents Henry has given you over the past five years. Finger your favorite, the gold silk shawl embroidered with parrots that he bought in Mallorca. He was there with Elaine on their twenty-fifth anniversary. She got Spain; you got a yellow shawl covered with bird claws.

All this walking has made you so thin. Study yourself in the mirror. Put on the lingerie Henry gave you and feel dismayed. Your breasts have deflated. They look like empty paper bags.

The lace scratches, but you wore lingerie because Elaine would not. You were always on the alert for the things she refused. She wouldn't give him head. She hated oysters, Henry's favorite food. So you pretended to love them. You sat on bar stools with him at Swan's on Polk Street and ordered dozens, though their slippery texture repelled, though the look of the shells on the chipped ice was appalling. You paid attention to what Elaine balked at, and you cornered that market.

Now the market is so wide: You are alive.

TABLOID

I know what they will say.

I can see it now, in the checkout line of supermarkets. The cashiers, young girls mostly, with blackheads spattered in a freckly way on their foreheads, hardly ever recognize me. Once, a girl with violet eye shadow looked at me thoughtfully. "Aren't you on TV?" she asked, handing me my change. Her pink metallic fingernails scraped my palm. "I know. Weren't you on some *Twilight Zone* episode?"

But tragedy has a way of hooking people back into memory; in the face of some grand failure, humiliation, or despair, you become a celebrity again (that twentieth-century word for the mysteriously famous, those who accomplish nothing or, more accurately, nothing for years). Whoever thought of the man who invented the Scarsdale diet until his lover, a prim school teacher, desperate, shot him in the heart? I have felt a certain thrum of the heart before in these checkout lines, seeing a photograph of some former star; the first thing I think is that they are dead.

I am not dead.

I know this rather than feel it. I do absent-minded tests on myself, not unlike the tests I used to do when I was a teenager to determine if I were crazy; on subways I would think, If the train stops on Seventy-first, where it never stops, I am insane. Now, I eat until my stomach hurts. I don't want to feel satisfied, or even stuffed; those feelings are too subtle for my nervous system to locate. No, I am like most musicians, half deaf from listening to loud noise too long, who must hear everything loudly to hear it at all; pain is the only feeling I can detect anymore.

Celebrities are confessionals. I speak this as a former celebrity, newly returned to celebration. We may insist on our love for privacy, but why else are we here, performing, shaking hands, smiling for photographs? We want affection, attention, we want to unburden ourselves. That is why to be suddenly forgotten is so baffling; no one wants to hear our stories anymore. That is why those child actors, plump, dwarfish, trying to whittle their adult flesh and bones and muscles back to the cuteness of children (collagen lip implants, tiny upturned noses, you know these tricks) hold up stores, with toy guns no less. They are not done playing, they remind us. They have more to say.

My ex-wife, Constance, has told me I'm bitter. I can't have it both ways, she said. I can't resent people for intruding and then for ceasing to intrude. She doesn't understand, I told her, though in fact she does better than most: She has been a celebrity in her own way for most of her life. When she was eighteen, working in a picture frame store, she went to a party and met a man, a famous actor. Ben was doing drugs to teach himself how to be contemplative, and she joined in. They continued to do drugs for years, contemplating, and married each other before they sobered up into the less introspective arena we call the "real world." He was my close friend. Until I fell in love with his wife, who had a sweet, meditative smile, and married her.

Constance is more brittle now, as if she has a hard patina. Since we got divorced, a Caribbean divorce, seven years ago, she has been dating men who are famous in more reliable ways, movie producers and record executives. I doubt she could love an ordinary man—what she once called, mockingly, a private citizen.

My mind weaves and weaves, making loops of smoke, dissipating. I can see that there is no coherence to confessing, no clear path; instead this confession will puddle out, flabby, sloppy, widening, like Alice in Wonderland, floundering in a pool of tears.

Out with it—for aren't I simply pretending to confess and actually filibustering; aren't these loops of smoke distracting pyrotechnics, attempts to delay?

Last winter my son, five years old, fell sixty feet from the raised arm of an amusement park ride called the Octopus. He was standing up to wave to his mother, Petra, down below, and he lost his balance. He fell on concrete and cracked open his head. The doctors said his brain swelled. Consider those words for a moment: His Brain Swelled. Try to visualize it. And you might understand why I only think in puffs of smoke, why I can't, by all means can't, *absorb*. Needless to say, my son died.

That is my story. You may have even read it. But that is not all I have to say.

☾

Wonder World is the name of the amusement park. It's a second-rate Disneyland. Instead of Mickey Mouse, its mascot or Uncle Sam or however you like to think of the people in six-foot-tall fuzzy animal suits, is Mark the Shark. Apparently, Mark is a good shark. On Saturday mornings there is a cartoon about Mark and his adventures (living in the deep sea, trying to convince other sharks not to eat human beings, whom he befriends). I had seen bits and pieces of this cartoon while orbiting around Max, making sure he drank his juice and did not spill Cheerios over the carpet. I had gotten middle-aged, you see, and protective about my wall-to-wall carpeting.

The rides in this park all have a vaguely maritime theme. The nauseous spinning cars are called the Whirlpool. There are three roller coasters, the Tidal Wave, the Titanic, and the Manatee. Younger children are not permitted on these rides. A wooden cutout of Mark the Shark stands up in front of laps of roped-off lines. Mark's fin is extended, and a wooden bubble emerging from Mark's mouth reads, "You must be this tall to go on the ride, unless you are accompanied by an adult. Sorry!" I have no tape measure with me, but I believe the insisted-upon height is about four feet.

One of these Mark the Sharks stands in front of The Octopus, apologizing, unheeded.

Max was (was!) big for his age, no doubt about it. In his kindergarten picture he stands in the back row with the tall children. But he was a five-year-old boy, and though I do not know his height in inches, I know he came up to my hips, the top of his head level with my belt. He was well under Mark the Shark's fin.

What I want here, as I am sure is obvious, is someone to blame. Not because I need a punching bag, someone to act out violence upon. But because I would like someone concrete to discuss this with. Mark the Shark's fin was well over my son's head. Max was five years old. He was shorter than the fin. These sentences revolve in my head, over and over. He was five years old; he was shorter than the fin.

Perhaps by having someone to whom I can voice these... not sentiments—more like observations, I would at least elevate the dialogue. I might be able to move into more abstract and complicated issues, such as, What is the relevance of a rule that won't be enforced? Did no one notice my son, much shorter than Mark's fin? Or did someone in fact see Max, standing in line, probably cutting in front of as many people as he could? And did Max look up and smile at that someone, pleadingly, winsomely? Max had a wonderful smile, which he manipulated to its best advantage. I myself have found it hard, even impossible, to enforce regulations that he smiled at. I have found myself ladling hot fudge sauce over banned scoops of ice cream. I would understand succumbing to Max's charm; I honestly believe this. But I would like to know. I would like it explained. I want to express my point of view.

And where was his mother, you are probably thinking. He was waving to her. Petra was standing at the exit, laughing at something her boyfriend was telling her. She did not see Max at first, though before he got on the ride she had promised him she would watch. Then something made her turn and look up and she saw Max, sixty feet in the air, standing up in his car and waving. She shouted for him to sit down. Lifting her arms, she motioned for him to sit down. Max probably though she was waving back.

Laughing at a joke her boyfriend was telling her; perhaps the same phrase has caught your attention. She was distracted.

But Petra is no good as a scapegoat. In fact I admire her honesty. She sat on a green vinyl hospital couch tearing a Kleenex to pieces and told me that she had been laughing at a joke. She had not watched Max, as she promised she would. It was brave of her to tell me. God knows I was acting crazy. She cried and said, "It was my fault," and for all she knew instead of reassuring her, I could have said "You're right," and thrown her out a window.

Petra is young, much younger than my ex-wife. Twenty-four or twenty-five. Her boyfriend is young, too, her age, which means half of mine, a wavy haired makeup artist I more or less like. He's always been friendly to me as I have gone in and out of Petra's apartment, picking up or dropping off Max. He suits her. They're both sweet, spacey kids who like getting stoned and taking nude pictures of each other. Petra tries to be sophisticated, but the truth is, while she pretended that taking Max to Wonder World was a drag, she wanted to go almost as much as he did. She would have gone on the Octopus with Max, but she had eaten cotton candy and a slushy and two chili dogs, and she thought the momentum of the ride, lifting up in the air and rapidly descending, would make her throw up. She never saw Mark the Shark, smiling and cautionary.

Yet Max was a cautious boy, almost comically so. Don't think I don't perceive the pathos in this, though I may only be able to glance at it sidelong. Don't think I don't hear the voice of a sanctimonious disciplinarian, with wagging finger and Victorian hoops, or her twenty-first century doppel-gänger, the school guidance counselor: A boy as cautious as that, as chary of trouble and risk, must have parents who have made him so. Parents so outlandish and unhealthy that Max, poor kid, made sure he had his daily Vitamin C (who else would?). And he wouldn't participate in the dares and double-dares of children, the brave feats. At the swimming pool, he watched other kids cannonball off the high dive, and even the low dive, with no trace of envy or desire. If anything, what was in his round blue eyes was concern:

He worried that these daredevils would hurt themselves. Children smashing into the pool water with loud belly-flops would make him shake his head, like a disapproving grandma: Kids these days.

What was he doing standing up in that car, fifty or sixty feet in the air? My careful, seatbelt-loving boy.

A child as security-conscious as that is a stranger to emergency rooms, and only twice in his ridiculously short life did I see my son in a hospital. The first time he was not even a day old. I went to the hospital that day, some five and a half years ago, with no plans of loving this boy. My heart, I thought, was steely. There had been some ugly business with Petra, who wanted money—who could blame her? Nineteen or twenty, with a high school degree, and not much of a means of making a living. Being pregnant is a job impediment if you're a model. And who could blame me, though I know they will, for not wanting to give her money? How was I to know Max was mine? Petra and I had a boozy weekend fling, hardly an affair. So yes, there had been some ugliness, though Petra is no keeper of grudges. She left a message on my voicemail when she went into labor.

When I first saw Max, it was through a glass pane. A nurse hefted him up for me to see; she smiled and winked, like nurses do to new dads in TV shows. Max was all wrapped up in white swaddling, and he looked to me like an ice cream cone, his big pink head the scoop. The other infants, with their sticky sealed eyelids, seemed like coma babies next to my guy.

Did I love him right away? I felt a deep interest in him. I wanted to know more about him. For the first time in years—for the first time since I had met Constance, really, and was just starting to know her, this wife of my friend:

looking forward to seeing her at this party or that, and then watching her across the room, in some short bright dress, watching the awkward way she smoked and watching her drink and the sheen that alcohol left on her lips—for the first time in years, a person seemed fascinating enough to me to be worth endless study. Max's domed head, the frightening softness of it, those unfused plates of bone; his lilac balls; the drum of his stomach; the mauve snail-coil of his belly button; his paw feet. All things about babies, not just their bodies but their belongings, have a charm just for being small. The tiny shoes. Then later, as they grow up a bit, their sports equipment: the miniature baseball gloves, the plastic Wiffle bats. Their coffins, let us not forget, which can make you actually gasp because they are so damn small. I see I've made a full circle here: Max was small, undertakers of the world, and Mark the Shark, and pimply kids manning amusement park rides. He was small.

I see this is more of a rant than a confession. At a party last week (yes, I am trying to go out), a woman I slightly know grabbed my arm. She is a little younger than I, and good-looking, yet her hand on my arm looked to me like the gnarled hand of Fate. She had a daughter who died of leukemia a few years ago, and she told me, "It doesn't get better. I kept waiting for it to get better and it doesn't. Give up on that." She said, "I remember lying in bed thinking about spring. I thought, wait until spring. In spring it will be better, everything will be growing, all that. But it didn't get better. It's only when you give up hoping to feel less like hell that at least you can stop feeling bad for feeling bad."

My two drives—wanting to talk and wanting to be sealed off from the world—are wholly incompatible. Even Petra, who, God knows, I should and must talk to, is unendurable.

She called me, weeping, the other day, furious at something her mother had told her: "You can have more children," this well-meaning, bone-headed woman had said. Yet it was hard for me to listen, for the thought that coasted through my head was, She's right. However tactless or inappropriate such a thing is to say, she's right. Petra is hardly more than a kid herself. I doubt that Max's dying has put a crimp in her sex life. If anything, she and her nice, dim boyfriend Robby probably go at it all the harder, weepy, soggy encounters, tears and snot mixed in with the usual bodily fluids. Not an uncommon thing, from what I understand: People come home from funerals and tear their clothes off, because sex is life, after all, this relentless mashing of bodies a way of kicking death in the teeth, of reminding oneself this is my body: It feels, it feels. Still, the picture in my head of Petra and Robby pawing each other is, frankly, unbearable, and though this girl is Max's mother and deserves all my pity and attention, I just have to get off the phone.

Why do I have a right to be heard, if I can't bear listening? Constance used to call me a selfish bastard and she knows me better than anyone, or at least, anyone alive.

For didn't Max know at least a side of me that no one, not even Constance, would see? I was a good father, I swear it, even if I cared too much about my carpeting, or let Max watch too much TV, the wrong shows, or was tired some-times—the body gets old, wears down—and wouldn't horse around with my boy. But I was tender with him, and taught him some useful skills, how to tie his shoes, for instance, or, more flashy, how to skip rocks, how to sing on key.

I am not trying to toot my own horn here, for I don't take credit for my fathering talents. It's as if Max parented me, in some way, as well, for only in response to my charming son did I become this other man, this man who smiled often (but only around Max), not-quite-me. And since he's died, I wonder if that man can exist anymore, or is lost, dead to me as well, just as a shadow requires an object to cast it. I have not whistled once, now that I have no Max to teach how to wet his lips and pucker them in just such a way.

This is not a dream, because I am awake when it comes to me. I am lying on my bed facing the ceiling, but not seeing it, as I find myself so often not seeing what I stare at. I have been thinking about the Kübler-Ross five stages of grief, trying to remember what order they come in. And each stage appears to me to be a room in an old-fashioned museum, where by standing in the center of the first room, you can look down almost the whole gallery. Behind me, denial, a dark, muffled room, full of coats. The room I'm in is anger, no surprise: The walls are padded, like the walls of an asylum. People here kick and rave. The color is the awful rusty orange of a rec room, and I want to leave here more than anything, but the room ahead of me terrifies. Full of lurid blue light, it has no furniture. People lie on the floor and weep. I see no exit from that room. Somewhere around the corner may be bargaining, but this stage has never rung true to me. It seems too literary for death. In there, I suppose, would be Faust, and my lawyer, Bernie, who thinks I'm a jerk, and various agents. This room would be full of the people I hire to do things for me, make deals, get me out of things, marriages, contracts, responsibilities. Because of them, bargaining, like whistling, is a skill I've lost through disuse. And I suppose somewhere out there is acceptance, but really that's probably not a room at all, so much as an exit door: Out of this museum into the bright, light world. As you leave they hand you a prize. And the prize I picture is a stomach churner: a white bundle, very portable. It takes me a second to recognize it is a baby.

☾

Constance has been on my mind lately, for reasons I don't completely understand and don't really care to examine, so I go to a party I know she'll be at. I have not been invited, but the hostess, a loud woman, greets me with open arms. Her arms are like the blades of a scissor closing around me, her eyes rapt. Most of Constance's and my friends withdrew from me after our divorce—I suspect the general consensus was that I treated Constance like crap—but this effusiveness doesn't really surprise me. I have become, in my tragedy, reclaimed.

I see Constance across the room, with Ted or Ed or whatever her movie-producer boyfriend's name is. Both are looking at me, Ted's usual look of dislike mixed with something else, curiosity, which makes his expression oddly complicated: He appears to be having gas pains. Is it my paranoia that Constance hesitates before approaching me? It is only when she is right in front of me that she reaches up, pressing my shoulders with the palms of her hands, a quarter-hug. I hug her back. She pulls away after a second.

"How are you?" She puts the emphasis on "are" that I've gotten accustomed to—How ARE you?—that strange emphasis intended to signal that this is no generic comment that we all make, but a serious question. It makes me wince to hear this woman, whom I was after all married to for fourteen years, say the exact same thing with the exact same interrogative inflections that the hostess just said. But I've become aware how limited and generic our language of condolence is. How many people, from the elevator boy at my apartment building to a perfect stranger who recognizes me when I buy a pack of Marlboros to my own mother, have said the same two words, "I'm sorry," to me? Countless, countless.

I shrug, not annoyed exactly but wanting her to see my expectations of her are higher, and that there is no answer to this question. She flushes.

"People ask me about you all the time," she says. "Everywhere I go people want to know how you are. As if I'd know. As if I talk to you every day."

Her face, twelve inches from mine, seems as complex as her movie man's. Her eyes are wary, sad, resentful. Maybe she's pissed off about that self-righteous shrug of mine, so, to make amends, I tell her, "I came here to see you."

Her mouth twists, and it strikes me that now I've presented her with a comment impossible to respond to: What's she supposed to say? Thanks? Why? "Huh," is what she comes up with.

Silence, both of us casting around for something to say. A bizarre experience, as we usually have no problem talking to each other. Constance and I have a very modern divorce, amicable, as they say. Our social scenes are mostly different—Con puts far more energy into her friends than I do, and maintains a much wider sphere—but on the occasions we find ourselves at the same gatherings, we often end up in a corner, talking. I always loved to talk to her.

"Listen, can we go somewhere for a drink?" I manage, finally.

She looks at me and then looks away. In a sudden panic that she'll say no, I add, "Please? I can't handle being in a crowd."

It's a manipulative thing to say, and I feel a little ashamed for it. Her gray eyes move back to my face, and she looks me straight in the eye, letting me know that I'm being manipulative. But again, it's an amalgamated expression: The last time I saw her was at my son's funeral, when her eyes were full of tears, making me think in my insane mindset of the time (everything surreal—the flowers appeared to be balled fists) of the runny yolks of some lightly-done sunny-side-up eggs. I am in some safe zone where no one is allowed to look at me with pure antipathy, and even now, Constance is on the verge of tears.

"Let me tell Ned," she says.

Victorious, I motion for her to retreat to her fat-cat lover, and she nearly speeds to his side. I turn my head so I won't seem to be openly staring at them, and through lowered lids watch them consult. He glares at me: My kidnapping of his gal has returned his expression to its simpler form of pure dislike. Constance is looking at me also. She appears to be almost frightened. I wonder what kind of figure I cut, in my scruffy clothes and unshaven face, ripping into a party only to haul off one of its guests. My focus has been on my evasive ex since I've gotten here, and it's only now that I notice half the party seems to be glancing in my direction. Constance comes back to my side, coat in tow, and I'm tempted to give these gapers a real show, sling Constance over my shoulder and gallop out the door.

We walk down the street. I've tucked her arm into mine and I think we look like an old-fashioned couple, heading perhaps towards a Broadway show. There's a bar at the corner which Constance tries to steer me towards, and I pass by. I'm afraid that she might have told her Ed that we'll be there, and I don't want him to charge to her rescue. We close in on a darker, smokier bar two blocks farther down. In the window, a neon martini glass, the olive a lurid loop. "Here?" Constance asks, tugging my arm.

"Too dirty. I have a place in mind," I say. Of course I don't—I just want to put some distance between us and my antagonist, Old Ed. Constance blows out an exasperated little sigh, one which having been married to her for all our years I am of course familiar with: the sigh that used to mean, Stop refusing to ask for directions, Why are you wearing that tacky yellow tie, I want to sleep so stop it with your talking, talking, and which now means, Where the hell are we going? Strangely enough, hearing her sigh makes me feel a sensation so foreign to me in these last narcotic months that it takes me a second to recognize it: I'm happy. And what makes me happy is that, for all her sighs, her pincer-grip on my arm, the theatrical glances she casts at each bar we pass, and pass, I feel certain that Constance can't resist me. Her feet may drag, her eyes may roll, but here she is, in tow, my constant Constance. I actually chuckle, and Constance says, sharply, "What?"

"I was thinking of how we got together," I tell her. "When Ben left us alone at the beach house and you kept saying No, we can't do this. And then we did. It was like that time we were hiking and you didn't want to jump over that crevice."

"That crevice," says my former wife, "was a hundred feet in the air. I can't believe that you're calling it a crevice. That, my friend, was two cliffs, separated from each other by a good three feet, that you made me fucking jump across."

"I jumped."

"You were stoned out of your gourd. I was completely sober, and I can't believe you made me do it." She shakes her head. "You're a scary guy, you know. You do stupid things and you make me do stupid things. And I don't see what that Evel Knievel stunt has to do with Ben."

But of course she does. I can tell from the way she pinches up her face that she's lying. It's a ploy of Constance's, to pretend to be dense. "My point is, you did jump," I tell her. "And at that beach house, for all your protests, you did jump."

"What are you saying?" She's starting to look really pissed off. "That I'm some kind of dog? I come running when you snap?"

"No, no. I just mean there are things you can't resist, even if you try to."

"Like old irresistible you."

"Like love. Forget it. Let's not fight."

For a block there's no sound from her but the hard clatters of her shoes. Then, she says, "I remember a lot of things from that day. I remember telling you I loved Ben and didn't want to hurt him. And—what did you say? You loved him too but we couldn't betray our hearts? Some such garbage."

"Oh, well," I say. "It was the nineties. People expressed themselves in silly ways."

"Selfish ways," she says. "I remember a lot of things about that day. I asked you to leave so I could pull myself together, so I could have some space to think. And you said—."

"Not unless you leave with me."

She nods, fiercely. "I remember you kissed my stomach and said you wanted to have a baby with me. You wanted me to have your baby."

I stop, as the saying goes, dead in my tracks, and Constance stops, too. When she's upset her skin goes spotty, pink and white: marbleized.

"Shit," she says. "What do you want from me, Toad?" (that name she called me, for unfathomable reasons, for years;

that I haven't heard her say for years). She sighs, a very different sigh—in tenor, in motivation—from her exasperated one. "I feel horrible for you. I do. But so ambivalent, too. I want to call you and then I don't. I'm not sure how drawn in I want to get. I mean—." She extends her arms. "My life is simple now, you know? No more *sturm und drang*. And how do you think it made me feel, after all those years together when you didn't want a baby...."

"Constance," I mumble. Words seem like physical shapes I must spit out, and carefully, for the letters are barbed and hooked. If I don't watch it, they will rip the corners of my mouth. "You didn't want a baby." There. Spat.

She shrugs. "Neither of us, then. But as soon as we split up, you have this kid."

"A mistake, you know that."

"But was he? Was Max a mistake?" Her eyes are running now. "No. I don't begrudge you him—God knows I feel like hell for you. I've cried thinking about him, and you, and Petra too, poor kid. But I cried when he was born, too. It seemed unfair. I know that sounds petty as hell, but I thought, why does he get to start over, and I don't?"

Tears run down her face in lead-colored streaks.

"Can we start over?" I ask.

"You mean a baby? Come on, my dear. I'm forty-five."

I put my arm around her and we start again to walk.

"Where are we going?" asks Constance, her voice hoarse.

"Tell me the highest place you can think of," I say. I want to perch myself in front of a window. Instead of having this jagged cityscape towering above us, I want to be in the tower, nested in the sky. I don't tell her I want to find another way to fall.

BE GOOD

Verb, imperative form. First known usage: said to him in the foyer, his hair still wet from the shower, his suitcase in hand, on his way to some business trip; the kids upstairs, gobbling Apple Jacks. Accompanied by her quick kiss on the lips to seal it: "I'll miss you. Be good."

Definitions:

1. Do not, on this particular trip, fuck some woman with auburn hair, one who will proceed, for several months afterward, to "Like" every comment you post on Facebook; to "Follow" your tweets; in short, to "Like" and "Share" and "Follow" you like some pliant dog (not our dog, though. God bless snobby, misanthropic Frito).

2. More generally: Do not fuck anyone at all! Of any body type, age, profession, or fluency in social media. Look at your hands: Insert them in pockets.

3. But if you are, indeed, foolish enough to let those hands wander: Do not leave traces.

4. For example, do not be so stupid as to leave condom packets in the suitcase you neglect to unpack, so your

wife finds them when she (lovingly, thoughtfully) sifts for dirty laundry, pungent socks.

5. Of course, avoid less material forms of evidence. Do not by any means accept the Friendship offer extended by the woman you slept with in Chicago. You have accepted too many offerings from her already! Do not put your wife in the position of wondering who the fuck this person is, splattering herself all over your wall with her afore-mentioned "Likes." Do not induce your wife (compulsively, reluctantly) to look this woman up.

6. Because to degrade your wife in such fashion involves (insult to injury) deflecting her rage onto some stranger (Brittany, Celia, Dee) instead of where it properly belongs, onto you. This may be convenient for you, but it is unfair both to herself and to her gender.

7. Indeed, following the slick scent of those "Likes" and "Shares," your wife recalls that misogynistic joke her first boyfriend Tony (a jerk, if extremely hot) liked to tell: "Why do women have legs? So they don't leave a trail on the ground like a snail." Your wife remembers cringing when this dude uttered said "joke" twenty years ago. Not to her—she was simply sitting there—but to his friend Ray, to whom Tony had just passed a red, loaded bong. An hour before, your wife had let Tony finger her; he had not, an hour prior, been so disparaging about pussies.

8. She remembers thinking, I really should dump this asshole. This memory feels unnaturally vivid, because currently she is contemplating the same thought about you.

9. Which is just to say: Remember your vows. Not merely the obvious one, already implied here, but the one you wrote yourself: "I promise to split the difference on the thermostat." Seven years ago, that vow made friends and family in the room guffaw. It made your bride, whom you liked to freeze to death, to the point that she had to wear socks to bed, laugh. Recalling it now, however, makes her cry.

10. So, remember your vows. Because before you leave her for a week on your trip, before you wander, but, she hopes, not *wander*, know when your wife says, "Be good," here is what she really means: Be good to me.

NEPENTHES

When I loved Dana, she taught me a spinoff of a category game my nieces play. Her version was more idiosyncratic. Instead of "If you were an animal, what animal would you be?" it was "If you were a kitchen appliance," "If you were a weapon," "If you were a verb."

For verb, Dana selected for me "persist." I regarded that as a compliment; I pictured myself as a knight, doggedly climbing over armored corpses on my way to her fortress.

The verb I chose for Dana was "insinuate." She didn't take offense, and I didn't mean to accuse. So what did I mean, exactly?

In my mind, the word was broken into its component syllables: in sin you ate. The image it conjured was of Dana, the first afternoon we slept together, kneeling on the bed, licking dark chocolate from her fingers. I'd come to the hotel room bearing gifts—chocolate dusted with sea salt, scarlet roses, champagne we drank straight from the bottle.

When she was a teenager, Dana had been a model of some note—on the cover of two magazines, doing runway shows in Milan—but it was not her looks I found alluring. Truthfully, I didn't find her beautiful. Her eyelashes were so pale she reminded me of a lemur, and her thinness alarming: Those bladed hip bones abraded me.

But I loved to play with her, in and out of bed, and I remember all the avatars she chose for me. Along with the verb "persist," I was a spiked mace, a cheese grater, an alligator pear ("So much more romantic than 'avocado'").

Now, in the lacuna Dana has left in her wake, I picture these analogues she had for me, and I for her. They spin slowly in the air.

There are predators who are attractive in order to warn away, like poison frogs—their lurid blue color telegraphs that nothing so visible could be safely eaten. Then there are predators whose attractiveness allures: flesh-eating flowers, meaty petals summoning intrusion.

Once things cracked between us, Dana threatened to kill herself. My parting words, unaware that they were such: "I wish you fucking would."

Her note left on the green-veined countertop read, "Never say I don't do what you ask."

Antifreeze is a dangerous poison, my sister tells me, because it's so sweet; that's why it must be stored out of inquisitive children's reach.

VERSION

I

"What do you want?" she asked him once when they were lying in bed. "What do I get to keep?" Other couples, they break up, and it's objects they dicker over: the music collection, the never-used china. But when one is sleeping with a writer, it's the memories that get divvied: Who keeps the kisses at the airport, who gets the seedy hotel with the fingernail clippings on the night table?

Of course she does not explain herself.

And they wrestle over his journal. When he is peeing, she lifts it out of his bag and tries to find the page he began to read her before stopping: "No, I can't share this with you." Something about them necking in the alcove at the airport. That was the word he used: necking, like a teenager, like a boy. She thinks of the supple muscles of his neck, his hot skin.

Then he is out of the bathroom, his hand on the door frame: "Hey! What are you doing?"

"Nothing. Go wash your hands, go brush your teeth."

He uncurls her fingers from the journal, holds it over her head, out of reach; he pins her arm behind her back.

"No, you don't." He laughs. "Stop kissing me, you don't get it back."

"But I just want to find the part about me. Aren't I allowed to find myself?"

"This version doesn't belong to you."

☾

They do not talk about what will happen after this year. Kate is a visiting writer, and the marks she makes at this school will leave no prints: footsteps in grass rather than snow. The tense he uses with her is present, and the direct objects he attaches to love are not herself: "I love your kneecaps, I love your carrot salad, I love the ink stains on your hands."

She first meets him at her job interview—not the formal part, when the search committee interrogates her, but later. He's sitting in the back of the room when she reads her story, and she sees him again when they take her to the faculty lounge. He's standing in a corner, looking at her, eating bright orange cheese cubes speared onto toothpicks. He has a whole handful of cheese cubes, and the first thing she notices about him is his open hand with toothpicks spiking out.

She approaches him (well, she tells herself that she's approaching the wine, and she does pour herself some in a plastic cup. White, so it won't stain her teeth).

"It looks like you're holding a hedgehog." She believes at first that she's merely thinking that line. But it turns out she has said it out loud, because he raises his eyebrows, laughs, and extends a toothpick-free right hand.

"I didn't eat lunch. I'm David," he says.

She takes his hand and it gives her a shock. She drops it. "Whoa. That hasn't happened since I was on a playground slide."

That shock becomes part of the story they tell to each other about their meeting: literal electricity.

He is part of the group who takes her out to dinner afterwards, but he is sitting at the other end of the table. The only time he actually speaks to her is when she comes out of the ladies' room and he's standing in the corridor. Then he says, "Are you one of those neurotic people who like to get to the airport really early?"

She's a little startled—she's just come out the bathroom, he's standing right there after not talking to her all night, and he doesn't open with "Hi" or indeed any pleasantry at all—but she says, "Not especially neurotic, I don't think."

"Well, I'll pick you up at your hotel at nine tomorrow morning, then. I'm your ride." He smiles. "I just finagled it."

"Um. Thanks."

He looks her up and down, in a kind of obvious, exaggerated, slow-mo way. "Actually, let's make it eight a.m.," he says.

And still she almost misses her plane home. As soon as she sits in his car, he grabs her hand, and the whole drive to the airport, except when he's signaling, he holds it. He puts the car in short-term parking to walk her in. But he doesn't touch her—it's still just their hands—until they approach the security line, and then somehow without exchanging any dialogue they end up kissing in an alcove, kissing and kissing until she says, "I'm going to miss my plane."

"I knew I should have given you a ride back to your hotel last night." He shakes his head and laughs. "Damn. What is this?"

"I have no freaking idea," she says.

"Do you make a habit of seducing prospective colleagues during fly-backs?"

"*Me* seducing?" she says. "Hardly."

"I don't know if I want you to get the job or not. You could be very distracting."

"Well, maybe you'll get lucky. Maybe they'll give it to the drunk."

"Or the lesbian." He kisses her again. "Run along. And stay in touch, you. Send me that story you were talking about last night. The one about the spare ribs."

"You were listening to that?" she asks, even though she knows—she could tell at the time—that he was.

She gets the job, though by the time they offer it to her, it's turned into another job entirely, whittled and shriveled. They lost the funding for the tenure-track line, so now it's a one-year gig. In fact the job is no better than the one she already has, and it's unclear to Kate herself how much of a factor the Hot Writer Guy is in her acceptance of it.

When she drives up to the house she has rented for the year (from a French professor, on sabbatical), David is waiting on the porch. He has a bulging bag of groceries with him—"Just some staples" he tells her, when she asks what is in it. And she laughs in the kitchen when she unpacks it, and finds among the milk, coffee, eggs, apples, sliced salami, cream cheese, and bagels, a box of staples. He stands behind her with his arms around her. He kisses the back of her neck.

"Let me at least shower," she says. "I've been driving for two days." But he shakes his head, he pushes her into the French professor's bedroom.

Later he asks her, "So how discreet are you? Because this sort of thing is frowned upon, you know."

"Very discreet," she tells him.

They are undercover, or so they think. He won't hold hands with her anywhere near campus, or any bar where they might run into students or colleagues. "Discretion, temptress," he says. But it occurs to her all this subterfuge might be an excuse.

She tries to explain it, him, to her friend Ellen over the phone: to explain it to herself.

"I'm regressing," she tells Ellen. "He's the type of guy I liked in high school. You remember? The two types: the tortured poet and the bad boy. He's like a smoothie blend."

"And you were finally growing up," Ellen sighs. Ellen had high hopes that Kate would fall for a doctor she introduced her to, a nice guy, divorced, responsible, cheerful, but that has all gone by the wayside in the wake of David. "Remind me what you see in him."

"Sex. Scrabble. The conversation. We can talk and talk."

"About what?"

"Oh, stupid shit. You know, what word belongs in this sentence? What color, exactly, is that mustard? Why did Freud screw up with Dora? Things no one would care about besides us."

"You're in love with him," Ellen says. "I can tell by the way you say 'us.'"

They carry on. "Carry on" is his phrase, and she asks him in what sense does he intend it? Carry on meaning to continue, or to fool around, or to have wild tantrums?

"The first two," he says. He looks at her speculatively. "You don't seem like the wild tantrum type."

She does her best to be cool, smooth, light. These are characteristics that Kate has always possessed, but because he approves of them, they become exaggerated. Sometimes Kate thinks those adjectives would better describe a product (a Scandinavian lamp, say, or a moisturizer) than a person.

When she asks him, "What's going on with us?" he evades her. He quotes Thom Gunn: "'Their relationship consisted/ of discussing whether it existed.'"

"Don't think so much," he tells her. He bites her earlobe: "Thinking again?"

But what is she supposed to think? For instance: She comes to his apartment a late May evening, knocks. He doesn't answer, so she feels for the keys he hides under a dented yellow watering can. When she opens the door, she sees them right away, sprawled on his ugly plaid couch. They haven't even made it into the bedroom. They are still wearing some clothes. She notes the girl has red hair, unshaved armpits, and is prettier and younger than she. His mouth is open, a round hole, and involuntarily Kate imitates it: "Oh," she says, before closing the door.

She does not answer the phone, though it rings and rings as she packs her books into orange and onion crates. She is glad she traveled so lightly. It would be easier to unplug the phone, perhaps: each time it rings she pauses in her packing.

Two days later there is a knock on her door. She doesn't answer. Her door opens anyway and he stands there. They look at each other.

"You know, in retrospect it was probably a bad idea to show each other where we keep spare keys," she says. "Give them to me."

He tosses them underhand. Kate catches them. She is very pleased: She can't think of a better occasion to make a graceful catch.

"Going somewhere?" he asks. She registers his tone.

Whatever he came to say has been diverted by the boxes.

"Nowhere," she says, and though they say more things, this is what she remembers, this is the clean cut she makes in the memory. He can have the rest.

The university tells her she must leave a forwarding address. She doesn't.

☾

Five years pass. She publishes her second collection of stories and goes on a book tour. Ann Arbor is her sixth stop, and by then she has a rhythm and a story she likes to read. It seems to go over well; it has lines that elicit reliable laughs, it's not too long, and the themes are easy to process in a sitting. The title is homey and sedative. But when she gets to the lectern, she sees him sitting in the second row, staring at her, and she changes her mind about what to read.

This is not the city where she knew him. It is a shock to see him, and she has to drink most of her glass of water to recover. After she drinks the water, she coughs. Then, without her usual jokey preamble, she says the title of what she plans to read: "This one is called 'Nowhere.'" In the front row she sees Ellen, her best friend, look up, surprised. She reads. It's a mean story, it has pointy teeth, and it's all there: the airport, the fingernail clippings, the journal, the yellow can. When she finishes reading, there is a pause before the audience claps, and their clapping is tempered. The professional in her takes note of this: "Black Tea" goes over better.

She takes her time signing books, chatting with each of the buyers, and he waits until the line is gone before he approaches. When he hands her one of her books, she signs it. Just her name. He looks at that part first.

"So," he says. He flips to the inside back jacket. "Vermont, huh? I wouldn't have guessed."

"And you live here?"

"Nowhere," he says, and smiles. "But now I have all sorts of information about you. You're forty-one …."

"You knew that."

"You live in Stowe, Vermont. Oh, and here's your publisher's address. Good to know. Nice picture of you, by the way; you haven't changed."

"Ha," she says.

He flips now to the dedication. "Who is Molly?"

"Me," Molly says. She has been sitting in Ellen's lap, in the front row. Now she disentangles herself and marches forward, sticking her stomach out.

He stares, then bends to his knees to look her in the face. "Hi, Molly. I'm David. Pleased to meet you."

"David?" Ellen repeats.

Kate gives hard looks all around, to Ellen, to Molly, to him. She deals them out like cards. Ellen stares back, eyebrows raised, but David and Molly ignore her.

"So, Molly," David says. "Who's your mommy?"

Molly points.

David turns to look at Kate, then back at the girl. "How old are you, pretty girl?"

"Four and a half," Molly says, at the same time as Kate says, "Three and a half." They say the word "half" simultaneously: it sounds like they are harmonizing. David looks at Kate, then her daughter, forward and back. There is a pause. The moment thins and contracts.

That is the lesson of fucking a writer. Everybody looks guilty.

II

Clean cut.

Or: there are different ways to proceed from here.

David walks out of the bookstore. He doesn't say anything, but the look he gives Kate is certainly legible: to hell with you. He goes back to his apartment (on Plymouth Road, some twenty-two blocks away; it takes him less than twenty minutes to walk there). He shakes his head most of the way. He is actually talking to himself; he is that discombobulated. Someone watching him on the street might conclude he's crazy (and indeed there is someone watching him, a nineteen-year-old girl with long dirty-blond hair and a crocheted hat. She's a philosophy major at the University of Michigan. She thinks to herself that he's cute but seems pretty weird).

He gets home, and the first thing he does is hide Kate's book, stuffing it behind other ones on the shelf so he doesn't have to contend with that spine staring at him. He pours himself a glass of Maker's. He thinks why the fuck did he go to that reading anyway? Idle curiosity, cats, there's a predictable narrative.

He takes out the book from where he shoved it (behind the E's, George Eliot, Ralph Ellison, Louise Erdrich. Kate was not the first to point out the disjunction between David's organized bookshelf and his messy personal life).

He reads the story, "Nowhere." It's rambling and ends, he thinks objectively, too abruptly, but there's a line in it that makes him smile: He remembers quoting that Thom Gunn poem to her. He remembers her reply, "He insisted, she resisted;/ so they persisted, misfitted." (She has left this comeback out of the story, though, and he isn't sure why:

If it had been his line, he would have kept it.) The way she would roll her eyes. Mocking, narrow, nearsighted eyes. They were the first thing he noticed about her.

David starts leafing through the book. He reads "Black Tea," but it's not his favorite. He likes one called "Convolutions" quite a bit, about a young pregnant woman who has an old, decrepit, needy cat. He wonders if she wrote it when she herself was pregnant.

He spends the rest of the evening reading the book.

When he's done he restarts his computer (it's close to midnight now) and Googles her for twenty minutes. She isn't on Facebook, either openly or surreptitiously, and her old email account doesn't work (he already knows this last bit), but eventually he finds her, "visiting" at the University of Vermont.

He writes: "well, that was very strange, and i'm having trouble figuring out exactly what to say to you. so two things for now: 1) "convolutions" is really strong, maybe my favorite story of yours, though i always liked that bizarre one about the acrobats. i love esp. the bit about the cat's greasy fur—you can almost feel it under your fingertips. 2) how long are you in town? because i'd like to take molly out for ice cream, if you'll let me. (and if you won't i'm prepared to make a fuss). needless to say, you're invited too. xo, d."

He hits "send" without giving himself the opportunity to reread, edit, delete.

☾

She doesn't answer. And in the end, despite his claim, he's not prepared to make a fuss. But he checks his email often for the next few weeks, and Googles her some more, and writes a letter (handwritten this time, on heavy, porous paper), which he mails care of her publisher. He writes it late one night when he's a little drunk, and drops it in the mailbox the same night, and in the morning he doesn't remember exactly what it said, except that it featured the word "regret."

☾

Or: She emails him back the next morning. "Hey mr. lower-case. Truth is I'm not sure exactly what to say, either, except that reading that story was probably bad form and I've been a little ashamed of myself. Molly and I are staying with my friend Ellen in Detroit. We leave tomorrow for another leg on this long-ass tour. Ice cream is out (she's lactose-intolerant), but if you can make it to Detroit tomorrow morning at 10 we'll meet you at the playground in Belle Isle Park. That's as much as I can offer. Kate."

He goes. He gets lost on the way, but he has given himself plenty of time to correct for mistakes.

He discovers that Molly is very charming, though he has never been particularly interested in kids. He attempts to teach her Twenty Questions.

Kate is not, at first, especially friendly. She is wearing sunglasses (it's cloudy) and she crosses her arms. He pictures her in a suit of gleaming, hermetically sealed armor. She hovers but does not facilitate conversation. She is not helpful, for instance, about explaining the rules to Twenty Questions. So he focuses on Molly.

But after David teaches the game to Molly (who calls it, simply, "Questions") and gives her some pointers for how to play, and Molly asks, as instructed, "Is it alive?" and then, when he tells her it isn't, asks, "Is it a dead bird?" David laughs, and Kate lowers her head and smiles.

Molly keeps guessing ("Is it a dead bear?" "Is it a dead caterpillar?"). The corpses pile up. At some point Kate removes her sunglasses. At some further point Kate says, "Hey. David, she's guessed about fifty things. What is it already? This is too hard for her."

"Give her a chance."

"It's too hard. She's only four."

"Four, huh? I thought there was some debate about that."

They study each other. Kate shrugs. "Come on, what is it? The answer?"

"It's a story," he says, finally.

She shakes her head. "First of all, way too abstract. She's never going to guess that. You have to play fair with kids, David, or they'll never trust you."

"Crap, you're right. Hey Molly!" he calls after Molly's retreating back, aimed now for the slide. "I'm sorry!" He turns back to Kate. "I wasn't thinking."

She nods. "Second of all, too general. The whole point is to be specific. Not 'a story,' but 'Snow White,' you know, something particular. Third: I thought you said it wasn't alive."

Now he's the one who can't stop himself from smiling.

She smiles back. "Cheater," she says.

He tries to describe her smile to himself, discarding one by one various adjectives: broad, sharp, knowing, reluctant, superior, amalgamated.

There are things about Kate (her eyes, for instance; her cleverness; a way she has of hugging herself, as if to keep herself intact) that he misses. It surprises him, how glad he is to encounter these things now.

☾

Molly is hauling herself up and then slipping back down the slide, over and over again, a miniature Sisyphus. Ten feet apart, they both face her.

"Let me check my 'watch,'" Kate says, making air quotes. She pulls out her cellphone.

"That reminds me: What's your number?"

"Wouldn't you like to know?" She smiles. "Oh, Lord, it's almost noon. I need to get going. We have a train to catch." She turns to him. "What?"

"Oh." David shrugs. "I was just trying to remember—."

"What?"

"Why I blew it with you."

"Why? Or how? Because I sure remember how."

He looks at her. "Yes, you've made that point. I've got a distinct visual on 'how,' thank you for that."

She laughs.

"No, I was thinking about why."

There's a pause. She waits, then shrugs. "Well, that's for you to ponder." Turning away from him, she calls, "Molly! Five-minute warning!"

"Maybe I'll write a story about it," he says.

Her look becomes more threatening. Now he laughs.

"Don't worry, Kate. It would only reflect badly on me."

She waits again. She is practically tapping her foot.

David says, "I'm beginning to think messing things up with you was one of my more stupid moves."

"Lots to choose from."

There's that smile again. Obnoxious? Challenging? "Hey, do you remember?" he says. "'So they persisted, misfitted'?"

Her mouth opens. She seems, for once, legitimately taken

aback. "I do." She shakes her head. "I mean, I do now. But I'd forgotten …."

"Hmm, I was wondering that. If you'd forgotten saying that, or just left it out, for some reason."

"No, no, I would have used that, definitely," she says. "How strange …."

"You had some good lines, Kate. Me, too."

"Are you talking about real life? Or in my story?"

"I meant real life, more."

She grins. "I was waiting for the critique."

He hesitates. "Oh, what can I say? The ending was abrupt."

"In the story, or in real life?"

"Both, I suppose. But I was talking about the story."

"But it was like that. As you just conceded. As you know."

"Oh, but come on, Kate." David extends his hands. "You teach this stuff. What's the first thing we tell the chickens in a workshop? It doesn't matter if it 'really happened that way.'" Like her, he indicates air quotes. "Who cares? What is real anyway? We're all trapped within our own subjectivities. The only thing that counts is whether or not it works in the story."

"So you think the ending sucked." Her face falls.

"Sucked isn't the right word."

"Too harsh?"

He laughs. "I was thinking, too juvenile! Let's see. I'm sticking with, it was too abrupt. That's my final and objective opinion."

"Ha! But maybe you're right." She frowns. "Molly, careful on that slide. Sit on your booty."

"Well. It's revisable."

"The ending? What do you mean?"

He smiles at her. Her eyes narrow.

"Come on. Ask me the question," he says.

"What question? I'm getting confused about all these questions."

He waits.

"You and your word games," Kate says.

"*You* and your word games. Come on, ask it."

She stares him down.

"Oh fine. You're supposed to ask—come on, Katie, you're supposed to say, Is it revisable in the story or in real life?"

"The story is *published*," Kate says, lifting her chin.

He laughs. "OK, OK. Though publishing isn't the final version, necessarily. Look at *Leaves of Grass*. Whitman messed around with that forever."

Tap, tap, goes her imaginary foot.

"Well, the truth is I was wondering about real life."

"Molly, on your booty I said!" Kate calls. "What are you talking about exactly, David?"

"'Nowhere.' Bad place to end. I'm wondering if it could end somewhere else. Just speculating."

"David. You're being maddening. Too vague."

She's standing perhaps ten feet away from him. He takes a step towards her. "I think you need to add another scene. At least one more."

She shakes her head. "The story's over."

"But didn't you say it was alive?"

"Seriously. Stop playing games with me."

"All right, all right, I'm being serious. I screwed up. Granted. I'm not trying to defend myself." He draws a circle in the sand with his foot. "What if, for instance, I came to visit you in Vermont?"

She is shaking her head, but somehow she doesn't convey "no." Not exactly.

"Well, then, what if I join you and Molly on the next leg of your book tour? I have six weeks before the semester starts. I can get away for a few days. Where are you going, anyway?"

"Nowhere," she says.

He rolls his eyes.

"Come on, David, you lobbed that one to me! Softball."

"Whatever. Let me come."

"What am I supposed to tell Molly?" she asks, after a pause.

"Whatever you want. If I start pissing you off, I can always drive home. If nothing else, you'll get a free ride to—where are we going again?"

She starts to laugh.

Another step. He is almost touching her now. "But Kate—do me one favor and read some other story."

"'Black Tea,'" she says, decisively.

"Really? I preferred the one about the sick cat."

"Not for a reading." She is shaking her head again. "Too much of a downer."

"Come on. You aren't there to entertain them. You're supposed to challenge them, to provoke them."

"Actually, I'm supposed to sell books."

In the midst of this argument ("That's facile"; "No, that's practical"), they smile. Something about this discussion feels, to both of them, very familiar.

III

Or: David goes back to his apartment. He does not email Kate, though he does, over time, read her collection (it takes him several weeks, because he keeps hiding the book from himself, like a tempting bag of potato chips). Naturally, she does not contact him.

Twenty years pass.

Molly grows up. She becomes, predictably, a writer. (Or maybe that isn't so predictable: maybe it would make more sense if she did something completely, aggressively different—like being a marine biologist, or a mechanical engineer. Someone who built tangible things instead of fantasies and dreams. However, in this version, she becomes a writer.)

Nonetheless, she is a writer with very different proclivities and ambitions than her parents. One knows there is something rebellious about this career choice after all by Molly's disdain for writing fiction. (Or, as she calls it, using air quotes, turning her pretty, painted index fingers into hooks, "fiction"). How she puts it, in interviews, is that all writers, so-called fiction writers included, exploit real life. None of their friends are safe, especially the epigrammatic ones. Writers plunder and appropriate, but the "fiction" writers dress everything in masks, glitter, and capes to create grotesque Frankenstein hybrids. The problem with creative nonfiction is that one's sense of reality is never, of course, reality *per se*, but nonetheless it's the more honest, aboveboard narrative form.

Her first book, published when she is twenty-four (by Harcourt, her mother's publisher— Molly is quite defensive about any alleged nepotism) is a memoir. The title is Plausible Deniability, and like the memoirs of others (one example Molly points to is Barack Obama's first book), it isn't principally about the parent who raised her but instead the one who didn't, the one who eluded her, and whose elusiveness made him, Karl Marx would say, that much more valuable. (That analogy is Molly's: Her book in different ways compares the family to the marketplace.)

Of course Kate is in there, too. The mother who is also a writer, who struggles and moves them and moves them again from one marginal college job to the next, from one summer writing retreat to another, publishing this and that along the way, to spare but mostly positive reviews and to not many readers, and then suddenly, with her fifth book, becomes quite famous. She's a finalist for the National Book Award and then wins a Pulitzer, and a job at a prestigious university (Brown) which she keeps for a few years before she surprises everyone, herself most of all—no, Molly most of all—by getting married at age fifty-eight and moving with her South African husband to Johannesburg. It all rattles Molly, but by then she is twenty-one, graduating from college (Oberlin), an official grownup herself, and already beginning to write.

Things of note about Molly: She seems older than she is. People are invariably surprised to learn her age. Her face is moon-shaped. She collects small, exquisite objects, such as antique buttons cut like rosebuds, cordial glasses, dollhouse pastries and condiments. At twenty-two, she has had one meaningful relationship, with a man five years older named Soren. Her friends on the whole regard Soren as a negative influence: Molly becomes more serious when they are together, even somber ("glum" is a word they use). She goes out with him for a little over a year, and breaks it off shortly after graduation, partly because she feels like she was always busy calculating exactly how much Soren loved her, so she could love him slightly less. She pictures his affection as a cup of sugar, and herself as reducing her return of it by two or three teaspoons. Molly is not the only one to believe that this preoccupied measuring has something to do with her parents.

The story of the title of her memoir is this:

When Molly is twenty-two years old, she finally tracks down her father. "Tracks down" is perhaps the wrong term, as it isn't as if his identity were a secret, or as if David were hiding exactly. Molly can't actually remember a time when she didn't know about David. (Kate, both the real Kate and the Kate depicted in Molly's book, is a long believer in answering children's questions honestly. This meant that Molly had a very graphic, technical, and precocious understanding of where babies came from, which is the subject of one of the funnier chapters in her book. It confuses Kate and hurts her feelings, though she would never tell Molly this, that one reviewer describes Molly's famous mother as "having no boundaries"). Nonetheless, Molly never approaches David until she is twenty-two. By then she has read all four of his books (one has done pretty well) and has been following him, at a distance, for years.

Although she is by then, or at any rate has resolved to become, a writer, Molly does not write David in advance. Nor does she call him. Instead she shows up at his door. She already has her memoir in mind by then, and may be thinking, if unconsciously, about dramatic effect, staging. She would not be the first writer to plot her own life.

David is shocked to see her, though not in the final analysis all that surprised. And he is polite, if not especially warm. He invites her in. He takes her coat (houndstooth, purchased at a thrift store. Molly has put considerable thought into what to wear). He offers her wine (Protocolo). He pours himself a glass of Maker's Mark.

"Plausible deniability" is his phrase, his response to a question Molly asks. She has of course heard Kate's version of the bookstore reading. She has heard it and solicited it and repeated it for years. It is the closest thing (except, perhaps, "Nowhere" itself) that Molly has to an origin story. As she gets older, she asks more questions, but Kate's story does not vary.

"Did he say anything? After 'How old are you, pretty girl?'"

"No. He just looked at you and then looked at me, and after a minute he got up and left."

"A whole minute?"

"Forty-five seconds, maybe."

"How did he look?"

"Like if his eyes were guns, he would have shot me."

"No, how did he look at me?"

"Well, baby, I didn't see from your perspective. I mean, literally, I didn't. I just saw the way he looked at me."

Eventually, Kate's patience wears out. She gets exasperated. She says, "I have nothing else to contribute here! Why don't you ask Ellen."

So Molly consults her godmother, whose version is more or less the same, except that it includes Ellen's own shock: "*That's* David? Really?"

What does Ellen mean by really? Was he disappointing somehow?

"No, not exactly," Ellen finesses. "It's just that David Constable had been so larger-than-life. Such a figure. And to encounter him in person—well. He was smaller somehow than the picture in my head. That might be a cliché to say, but there you go, and clichés after all exist for a reason. He was wiry. He had black, curly, crazy hair."

"Like mine?"

"Yes, Honey. And intense eyes. I remember that. But I can't remember the way he was looking at you, exactly. I was so shocked, myself. I was staring at David more than, you know, evaluating his expression. Just trying to absorb it all."

(Ellen is not a writer. She's a neurologist. This is not the first time Molly experiences her narrative powers, particularly of description, as inadequate.)

One thing Ellen confirms, though, is Kate's rendition of the dialogue. "She said 'three and a half'; you said 'four and a half.' I remember thinking, 'Oh, fuck.' He did not say anything—anything at all—and after a minute or so he walked out."

"A minute or so?"

"Maybe two minutes. Molly, it's not like I had a stopwatch! He walked out and that was the end of it."

Molly feels as though she has spent her entire conscious life dissatisfied with this particular ending.

So she shows up at his door, age twenty-two, wearing her perfect, hipster, lavender-and-chocolate brown houndstooth coat, and accepts a glass of wine, and he pours himself a bourbon, and they sit there, staring at each other (Molly on a plaid, scruffy couch, David in a rocking chair), and she asks him. What was he thinking? Why didn't he say anything? And his answer, after a pause, is "Plausible deniability."

If he left then—right then, without pursuing it, without getting to the bottom of it, without receiving a final answer to his question about Molly's age—well, the question was left open, correct? Unresolved. He could choose to believe Kate ("three and a half"). To accept Molly's version ("four and a half"), well, that involved fucking up his entire life. There are certain people who just shouldn't be parents. Who never intend, if they're responsible and at all self-aware, to be parents. It was easier, for these reasons and others, to end the conversation then, though of course he could appreciate how, from Molly's perspective, such an ending would seem premature, too abrupt.

"But what *did* you believe?" Molly presses.

"Oh. That you were my child, of course. I mean, look at you."

Molly reflects, then repeats his words. "So 'plausible deniability' for whom, then?"

David shakes his head. His hair, curly as hers, is mostly gray. "For myself, of course. So I could maintain to myself that who knew? So I could walk away."

Later—but not a long time later, for the entire visit lasts fifty-five minutes—he asks about Kate, and Molly tells him about South Africa, the three teenage stepchildren, Kate's new interests (gardening, conservation). He nods. He knows all this already (well, not about the gardening, but who cares about that, really).

"I've kept up with your mother over the years," he tells Molly. When she opens her mouth with surprise, he waves his hands. "Oh, not kept up, kept up. Not with her personally. I mean I've kept up with her work." He gestures towards his bookshelf, and there she is, Molly sees, next to George Eliot. "I've read all of her books. She's done very well for herself, your mother. Though I will say that I didn't love that book that was so celebrated. You know, the one that won the prize. I like her earlier work more. There was a story about acrobats I really liked."

"'The Contortionists.'"

"Yes. A fine, fine story."

There's a pause, and then Molly makes herself ask the other question on the top of her list. "So why did things end with you and Mom? Your version, I mean."

He is silent for a minute. "You know, I really liked Kate. She was smart, and funny, and we certainly had what I suppose you'd call chemistry. The first time we touched, she actually gave me a shock."

Molly nods and smiles. She knows that already.

David nods, too. "Oh yes. That was in that damn story, wasn't it?" He shakes his head. "Well, I suppose the real issue was we didn't define things very clearly. We never had that conversation—you know: Is this exclusive? What are we exactly?"

"Were you seeing other women the whole time?" Molly asks.

"God, no. Is that what your mother thinks?"

Molly shrugs. "I think she wonders."

"She might have asked me." He shakes his head again, frowning. "No, that was the first time, actually. She was a girl who worked at a café I used to go to sometimes. No one significant. I don't even remember her name." He stops. "Well, that isn't precisely true. Her name was Allison. But I only remember that because I have an excellent memory, not because she was at all relevant. That is, it's emotionally truthful to say that I don't remember her name, even if it's not factually correct. We would chat about jazz sometimes. She liked Coltrane. Again, I remember all this because I have a first-rate memory, not because it mattered to me. So, we slept together twice. The second time Kate walked in. It never happened again. After Kate left, after that whole incident, I avoided Allison. Shame, because I did like that café."

"But why?" Molly says.

David laughs, a little ruefully. "That's what children always ask, isn't it? 'Why?' I can't give you a better answer. She—Allison—she was sexy. She flirted with me. Kate and I didn't have set rules. I wasn't cheating on her, not technically. I know she saw it that way." He leans forward. "You know, if I could do it all over, I would, Molly, on several grounds. I did care about your mother, more than I even realized at the time, more certainly than she realized. But she never gave me a chance to explain. She didn't answer the phone. When I went to talk to her, she wouldn't listen. I tried to tell her then, but it was clear from her face that she wasn't going to hear anything I had to say."

"What were you trying to tell her? That that girl didn't matter?"

"Well, the correlate. That Kate did. Matter, I mean. I suppose if we're being precise …." He pauses.

Molly, leaning towards him, practically slouching, now sits up straight. She thinks that this is it. This is how investigative journalists must feel, or policemen during an interrogation when they finally get the criminal to crack or fold or whichever verb applies. Overall this conversation has not been quite what she was hoping for. David has been fairly candid, but she hasn't heard anything she didn't suspect or know. The information that the girl was a one-off is a little noteworthy, but she isn't convinced that it's true. At least that's what Kate would say: She'd roll her eyes and ask why Molly was taking his word for it. So far, this talk been more like a fact-check than a heart-to-heart. But now: She wishes she had a pen and paper, a tape recorder, even a camera crew. (She had considered the first two but rejected them as too conspicuous, too threatening.) A camera crew most of all, because she'd like to show Kate a film of this, to say, See, Mom? He's not a bad guy. Look at his eyes. You can tell he's being genuine. You can tell he's sorry about, well, everything. And just as quickly Molly discards the fantasy camera: No, it would be better after all if she wrote all this down. For herself, for Kate. Better if she mediates this. She can describe everything to Kate: David's expression, his furniture, his two-day beard, his nervous hands, his reserve that is, finally, eroding.

And it could be (Molly thinks later) that David senses all this, that he sees her sit up straighter, that he sees these ideas flash across her face like those old-fashioned flashbooks with the cinematic stills: the horse galloping, the daughter plotting, mentally organizing her book. Because instead of continuing ("carrying on," Molly edits later), he stops and looks at her sharply and says, "Forget it."

"What?" Molly says.

He sits up straighter, too, as if imitating her. "So you're my daughter," he says. "I accept that. But really, this conversation—this hypothetical conversation, I should say, because it never in fact occurred—doesn't concern you. It's between me and Kate. I went over there that day planning on telling her some things I thought I needed to say, and she wouldn't listen to me. Had she listened, it would be a different story. Then maybe all of this would concern you, would involve you. But as it is—" he shrugs. "If she wanted to hear what I had to say, she should have listened at the time. There are no rewinds."

"You could explain yourself now," Molly coaxes, but it's the wrong thing to say. He looks at her and she can tell he's imagining Kate there, behind her shoulder. The image (the projected image) galls her, because Kate has nothing to do with this: Molly is not Kate's puppet, grilling David at her instigation. On the contrary. Kate was never supportive of this whole plan. When Molly first told her about it (they were sitting at Kate's table in South Africa, the one with the deep knife grooves; Kate was wearing a long white blouse that looked like tissue), Kate's mouth was set, wary, downturned. But she restrained herself from much commentary, limiting herself to saying, "That man has a way with words."

David shakes his head. He gets up and pulls down a book from a shelf. It's the short story collection. He opens it to the title page and hands it to Molly, who looks at her mother's signature.

"When she signed the book at that reading, that's all she wrote: her name. We were together for almost a year. More than a year, if you date it to that job interview. And that's all she had to say. To me, I mean. Of course she had plenty to say about me. But *to* me: That was it." He looks at her. "Well, Kate always believed in reciprocity."

And after that, their conversation, truth be told, winds down. Molly asks for more wine to prolong things, and David pours it for her. She planned this visit to be a longer one. Well, she had different scripts. She knew it was possible that he could simply close the door in her face. She had been prepared for that. Of course, the best possibility was that they would click, they would connect very naturally, this would be the first step. Later, they would share work. (In fact, allowing for this trajectory, she has a story in her bag that she has brought to, possibly, show him. Like her coat, she chose the story very carefully.)

But in the end, it is a strain to fill a whole hour. Molly catches herself watching the clock. She has so many questions, she came here with so many, and now she can't seem to remember them, or they lead to nothing, they go nowhere. His answers are polite, but as brief as if he were being deposed: "No, never married. Not suited for it, truth be told." "The first two *Godfathers*. Those and *The Third Man*." "My favorite city? Prague, I suppose." "At this stage of my life, Kafka."

Don't you want to know anything about me? she thinks, but she cannot bring herself to ask.

Molly sips, fidgets, and deflates. It will take a lot of work, after all, to convert this scene, through the alchemy of writing (shit into elixir) into the denouement Molly requires.

MRS. WHITE IN THE BALLROOM
WITH THE LEAD PIPE

What you do is text, text, text. We're playing I with the girls. You can't be bothered to help Ruby hold her cards in a fan because you're too busy fiddling with that damn phone. "Matt, will you please," I say again, and when you look up, "Will you please help Ruby with her cards?"

"Oh, right," you say, and Tess elbows me and laughs. Silly Daddy.

But I know that stupid look is a mere Japanese mask for the fucking-around look, I can see it underneath like pink, burned skin under sunscreen. So I send you to the kitchen to make us possible murderers some cinnamon toast. While you're looking for the bread ("Matt, it's in the refrigerator"), I help myself to your cell. Tess sees me, of course; she's like her mom, she doesn't miss a trick. But I hold my finger to my lips; we're playing another game. My smiling girl eliminates a weapon from her sheet. I scroll through your phone.

Ruby drops the candlestick. The card lands like a roof on her sippy cup.

Here's what I wish: that I could smash your head, which you've shaved to pretend that going bald is a choice you're making; that I could splash something stickier than apple juice all over the floor. Except guess who would have to clean it up?

SUGARMAN

We all shared Sugarman, the same way we shared things when we were little: Bina's T-shirt with the apple in red sequins, Phyllis's fingernail polish, my white Gogo boots, Tiny's skateboard that gave us all identical scraped knees. We shared him and we ruined him, just like all those possessions.

His real name was Arturo, but we called him Sugarman, because he was sweet. Sweet to look at, and a sweet boy, too: even though he was on the basketball team, and friends with all the assholes. But he'd say sweet things. Not just, "Girl, you look fine," but also, "I like what you said in class, about that girl who Odysseus chucked like she was garbage. That was cool."

He made you feel smart. Though a little guilty, too, since we were already calling him Sugarman, and planning to junk him just like that girl Calypso.

We were an all-girl Justice League.

Bina had him first. By ninth grade she had the biggest boobs in the class. They were shaped like bells and bounced. Hell, even the three of us liked to play with them. At sleepovers we'd take turns being the boy, "I'm Sugarman now," kneading those pillowy breasts. Everyone got something out of them but Bina, who said they might as well be elbows, they did nothing for her.

For September and October, 2010, Bina gave Sugarman access to her boobs, and the rest of her. Then she cut him off.

That's how we planned it. Because that's what guys did: Odysseus and the rest of them. They stopped dropping by. They stopped calling. They stopped sending the child support, so for weeks all Mom and Benny and I ate were rice and beans.

My turn next. My superpower was reassuring. Easy to cultivate that art if you're the daughter of a drunk. I knew all about nodding, and massaging a head, except instead of "Poor Mama," it was, "Oh, that sucks," and "Taylor sounds like a real tool," and "Remember you're better than them."

And the truth is, he was; that part was true.

I fucked Sugarman, too. Then, one day, I said, "You're so boring." That was my Supergirl punch to his gut.

Tiny looked like she was twelve, but she was all muscle, sinewy and limber as a snake. She'd wrap her legs around a boy and it was like Wonder Woman's lasso, her grip. She had Sugarman in her thrall, even more than Bina with her magic goddess breasts. The month Sugarman was with Tiny, he'd come to school sweaty and dazed, like he had a fever.

We all had our favorite features of Sugarman.

Bina liked his hands. She said they were so warm and deft, those hands, they almost woke up her sleeping boobs. I loved his eyelashes, me with my practically non-existent, white-girl eyelashes. His were the effect I was after with my mascara wand, but could never achieve. They were thick and pointed like thorns. Tiny said his fine ass! Phyllis said his heart. But she didn't say it in a sentimental way; she said it like she was a voodoo sorceress, and she was going to eat the damn thing.

Phyllis was the one who broke him that spring. Her

power was her eyes: black and bottomless, like those hungry kids on subway posters. Phyllis was hungrier than any of us, even though I was dead sick of beans. She wanted to eat the world.

For two months, every time you saw Phyllis, she was wound around Sugarman. They were like two strands of a churro.

But one morning, we came to school, and Phyllis was wrapped around Donny Atar instead. For a second I thought Donny Atar was Sugarman, I was so used to seeing Phyllis's hands in the pockets of his black hoodie. No explanation, no warning. When Sugarman got to school, he couldn't believe what he was seeing. He said "Phyllis," but she just turned and walked away, Donny Atar's hand in hers. Donny looked back, a little sheepish—he was on the basketball team, too, he and Sugarman were friends, in a way—but Phyllis never did.

We felt sorry for Sugarman, after that. We tried to talk to Phyllis.

But she reminded us of our project. She reminded us that all men are dicks. Men throw women away like empty milk cartons. They don't send checks, they finger you when they are supposed to be babysitting you, they break your St. Bernard piggy bank and steal your Christmas money. Sugarman may be sweet now, but just you wait. We were the Amazon Justice League and they were the Menemy. Her eyes were hard and shiny, like the obsidian we looked at in geology, the rock with the glassy planes.

For a week Sugarman came to school, his long-lashed eyes so red and sad. Phyllis deleted all his texts. Then he disappeared. It was the end of his sophomore year; he was old enough to drop out.

That was four years ago.

Since then, Bina joined the Army, which surprised the shit out of us. I get letters from her sometimes, on thin airmail paper. "It's freaky here," she writes.

Tiny dropped out of school the end of junior year, when she got pregnant and decided to keep the baby. I still see Tiny, when she can get her mother to watch Jordan. Babies stress me out. Tiny comes to my apartment and we have a beer.

But Tiny's gotten weird. She told me a couple of weeks ago that she's thinking about becoming a man. In some ways that isn't a surprise; when we were kids, Tiny wouldn't let anyone call her Tiffany, and she used to pee like a boy, standing up. She said, "I want to get my boobs removed." I thought, What boobs? She never really had any. When I asked her why, she wiped her mouth with the back of her hand and said, "Men have all the power."

I could see her perspective—she was worn out and skinnier than ever, from looking after Jordan—but I wanted to say, Jesus, Tiny, don't you remember Sugarman?

Funny: I was the worst student of the four of us. I flunked algebra; I had to go to summer school. But now I'm the only one going to college. I'm thinking of being a nurse some day: it's good money and there's always a need. The trouble is I don't like the way sick people smell.

Phyllis was the smartest, but she never came back to school after junior year, and stopped answering our calls. It's heroin. Sometimes on my way to class I see her sitting on the sidewalk on the corner of Capp and Fifteenth, with her eyes half closed and white buds in her ears. Once I touched her foot with my foot and said, "Hey, Phyll," and she looked up and nodded.

But for a second it seemed like she didn't recognize me.

It was the strangest thing, because for that same second I didn't recognize Phyllis. This girl I'd known for nearly twelve years, bitter and jagged, and now her eyes were so peaceful. I almost bailed on organic chem. I almost stretched out next to her and said, "Give me some of that."

She was sitting on that pigeon-shit spattered sidewalk like it was a white beach in Bermuda. I wanted to sit on that sand with her and stare at the bright water.

Bina's uncle Muktar used to give her a Jolly Rancher every time she saw him, and she'd share it with us. We would taste watermelon but also the inside of each other's mouths. It was good luck, to be the one who had it melt on your tongue. Sugarman was like that piece of hard red candy. The four of us sucked him until he dissolved.

640

This is how Jane finds out Charley, her ex-lover, is sick: when Marybeth, the department secretary, sends an email to "humfac," all the Humanities departments (English, History, Philosophy, Modern Languages, Women's Studies, and Ethnic Studies, merged into a Hydra whose multiple heads keep gnawing its shared shoulders).

Jane deletes most of Marybeth's emails. She only opens this particular email because of the subject heading: "Update on Charley."

She reads it, then rereads it.

Charley is out of surgery. He is resting. Vivian thanks everyone for the lovely flowers.

Jane pictures Charley's wife Vivian: her long, muscular neck, which reminds Jane of a horse with a chestnut coat; her tony, Katharine Hepburn-ish voice; her blue-edged nostrils. She pictures Vivian so she won't have to picture Charley, lying in some hospital bed, IV tube biting his hand.

By the time Jane opens the email, the thread is already snake-long: "So glad to hear the surgery went well!" "Love to Vivian!" From Eloise, the dimpled medievalist: "Our prayers for them both." In Jane's secular department, only cancer activates talk of prayers.

Despite Jane's efforts, her imagination cannot avert from Charley's body.

She remembers lying in bed with him, three years ago, the first time they had sex, and seeing, on Charley's rib cage, that strange scar: as if someone had taken a cherry-pitter to his torso. Her trailing finger lingered there; she looked at him questioningly. He looked back, not saying anything, and then, finally, "Subdermal melanoma. It was five years ago." He leaned over, rapped the headboard with his knuckles.

"You never said."

"Well." He is from New England, not Vivian's manicured Greenwich, but Maine. He is reticent. As a couple, handsome and tweedy, Vivian and Charley always struck Jane as some bare rock promontory, just visible from the shore. Holding his hand, curled into a loose fist, Jane pictured herself as a black, glossy seabird, perched precariously on that rock.

He kissed her. "Afraid I'm going to die on you?"

In her office, sun slants through the window, spotlighting swirling motes of dust.

Jane remembers their first afternoon together, mixed, like the dappled wall of her office, of the joyful and the somber. She remembers the way Charley's fingertips lingered over her own scar, the keloid on her shoulder from the teeth of her neighbor's Doberman. In an email she sent him that night, she wrote, "I feel comfortable showing you my scars." And he responded, "I love scars. They show you've lived."

How can Marybeth's email be the way Jane discovers he is sick? Not just sick, but if the cancer has returned, likely dying? Surely this qualifies as the kind of emergency to end the embargo on email that is not strictly business related, soporifically dull? They had promised ....

Well, they had promised many things. They made promises in conflict with earlier promises ("Don't fall in love with me." "I will never mess up your marriage." "This is separate, just us." As if hotel rooms with their padded beds represented their own rocky, salted islands).

Jane looks at her watch: two fifty-five. Her survey begins in five minutes.

She gathers her anthology and lecture notes and stuffs them into the leather satchel that she bought eight months ago when she and Charley agreed to part—such a mature phrase. The bag was a treat, because she required comfort. Later: brownies, fancy stockings, a one-night-stand, too much wine.

She walks to class quickly, but also carefully, because she is wearing her painful shoes, camel and bone, that she wears only on Wednesdays, when they have divisional meetings. Charley once unbuckled the strap and said, "My God, these are sexy."

She is two minutes late to class. Jane registers her students' disappointment when she walks in. She knows not to take personally their resistance to being in class on a sunny, April afternoon. She puts on her reading glasses, which she doesn't like, because they are silly, and red, and make her look owlish (but she has not made time to get proper glasses because the optometrist, unlike satchels or ham-and-cheese croissants, does not qualify as a treat).

But then she takes them off, because she knows this poem by heart.

Charley's favorite poet and her own, the first thing they connected over, years ago, long before kisses and hotel rooms and promises-in-conflict and then withdrawals and silence. This is what she misses most: not being in his arms, but reading aloud Emily Dickinson. Seeing him shake his head in wonder.

Reciting poetry is Jane's party trick. The students, a moment ago disappointed to see her walk in after all, scuttling their half-formed fantasies to smoke pot and throw a Frisbee around the well-kept green, look up. They watch her eyes wander over their faces. Of course, she is not really addressing them: She speaks to Charley, wherever he is.

"I could not die—with You," Jane says. She pictures the line on the page. She visualizes Dickinson's dashes, so much stranger in manuscript: There, the lengths vary. Some dashes go up, some down; some look like raised swords. She pictures the uppercase Y of "You." Months later, she will think of this poem as she, neither Charley's wife nor widow, sits with bowed head at his funeral, in the back row.

Composing herself. Recomposing herself.

WHAT SHALL WE DO
NOW THAT THE MUSEUMS ARE CLOSED
AND PARIS IS BLUE?

The girl flies to Paris in the middle of June. In California there is a drought. The fountains of her school are empty and stand dry and steaming in the sun. Baths and dish washing must be regulated. But in Paris it is raining, raining when she pulls her suitcases through the airport's sliding glass doors, and as her taxi moves into the city limits, and she looks up at the sky and hopes this will mean change.

In March, Paris was sunny and the sky the deep, wet blue of the ribbon of tinted glass at the top of car windshields. Women carrying their baguettes would smile at the girl in line at the tabac and say, with un-Parisian friendliness, "*Il fait beau.*" She was in Paris then with a boy she was a little in love with. They had come there from three months in England, where the consistent rain had passed from novelty to cliché to a kind of omnipresent reality as tangible as the stone buildings. Now, sitting in the taxi with her purse heavy and smooth on her knees, she watches the rain with quiet complicity.

Outside her mother's apartment, the girl pays the cabbie. She pushes the buttons of the code and when the gate opens with a releasing click, she pulls her suitcases into the courtyard. Her mother is sitting on the window ledge of the front hall. The girl sees her with her face bent and her hands working, doing needlepoint, and calls, "Mom, it's me." Her mother looks down and waves, and in a minute she comes downstairs to open the inner building door. The doors in Paris are abundant and strategically arranged.

They hug each other lightly. "I heard someone, but I thought it was too early for it to be you," her mother says. They carry the suitcases up the stairs to the apartment.

The girl pours herself coffee from the warmer, and takes her cup into the front hall to sit with her mother.

"Rose left a week ago," her mother says, crossing her legs, "And Holly comes at the end of the month. I will see all my little girls again. We will be a real family, like on T.V."

The girl watches her mother's hand move up and down, dragging colored silk. Her mother mentions the name of a friend of hers, American, a former politician, who will be arriving that afternoon.

"How long is he staying?"

Her mother laughs. "Until he gets bored. You know him."

"That will be nice for you, to have a friend here," the girl says. Her mother writes often, and her letters are full of how lonely she is, how impossible the French are, how difficult it is to be in a country where you say, "I am isolated in my head," and people think you have made a grammatical mistake.

"Do you have any friends coming to visit this summer?" her mother asks.

The girl shakes her head no. Then she says, "Well, Jason might come to Paris. But it won't be to see me."

"Will you see him?"

"If he's here."

Her mother has a line about ex-boyfriends that she has said, with varying degrees of heat, for years: Why would I want him for a friend? Friends are people I like. She repeats it now.

"Well, anyway," says the girl. She takes a package of cig-arettes out of her purse and lights one.

"I just don't understand the point of seeing him," her mother says, knotting the thread.

"You used to like him, remember."

"That's the problem with Jason. He's likable. If he wasn't appealing, you never would have fallen for him." She looks at the girl and relents. "Can I have a cigarette?" She lights it with an odd delicacy. "I haven't had a cigarette since you were here in March. I was making fun of people who smoked."

☾

The politician arrives at four. Her mother goes to meet his train. She did not meet the girl's plane, but she explains that the politician is notorious for his incompetence in practical matters, such as taking subways and finding addresses. When they enter the apartment, the girl, who has been lying on the couch reading, puts down her book and lights a cigarette.

"What are you reading?" the politician asks. The girl has not seen him since he lost his final election, and he is a little older looking and a little heavier.

She shows it to him: *The Book of Laughter and Forgetting*.

"What do you think of Kundera?" he says. "I like him. I think he romanticizes himself as a womanizer, and his heroes are all womanizers, like Hemingway's heroes all walk away in the rain with their collars up. But I like him."

"It's a pretty bleak picture of married life," says the politi-cian. "Women hurt and men hurting them without intend-ing to. I think it's very true."

"You've never been married, though," her mother tells him. "I liked being married. You build a family together. Families are the only things that make sense. You have a family and that is a reason to live."

"Then name me a marriage you have ever admired," he says. "I cannot think of a single marriage I like. Marriage, commitment, are like that scene in *Star Wars*: walls closing in on you."

"I can think of marriages that work for both their partners."

"But one you yourself would want to have?"

"No," her mother says slowly, and, though she is often complacent in her cynicism, this seems to make her sad.

"Let's appeal to the young," says the politician, and looks at the girl. "Do you want to get married?"

"When I'm thirty-eight," says the girl.

"Do you like the idea of marriage?" His eyes, which are dark and large, bore into her.

"Come on," she says. "I'm twenty. I'm too young to be jaded."

"You read Kundera," he says. "You don't necessarily have to experience disaster to be jaded. A good imagination, which recreates disaster, will do the trick. Or simply a good education. Being young doesn't make you safe."

The girl looks at her mother, who thinks of herself as jaded, and who watches the politician with bright eyes and a flushed face. For years, the girl and her sisters have thought that their mother is in love with him, for she is happy and self-conscious when she is with him, like a girl on a date. Right now her mouth is wide, as if she is about to laugh.

☾

In the morning, the girl wakes up to find her mother gone. There is a note on the hall table that says, "Out to get croissants from the damned French." Her mother has a long-standing, though mute, feud with the man at a nearby patisserie. She insists that he deliberately gives her burnt croissants, and she repeats this to Americans at cocktail parties, all of them united by their perception of themselves as victims in hostile territory, recipients of the sourest oranges, the hardest cheese.

The girl finds her keys and walks along the Seine, looking for coffee and a tabac. The streets are white in the still-early sun. Not many people are walking by the river. When she is alongside the Place St. Michel, she walks across the Seine to the Île de la Cité and sits on a bench facing Notre Dame. The pigeons scrabble in the courtyard, their fat, soft bodies flashing blue. She lights a cigarette and looks at the cathedral, which she has always preferred from the side: There it is a giant spider, crouching on the sharp legs of its buttresses, the round windows as opaque as eyes.

In March she sat in the cathedral with Jason. It was his favorite place and she used to go there with him with patronizing good humor. They sat on the stone floor for an afternoon. It was dark and cool and the stained-glass windows splayed reflections on the floor like a gasoline rainbow. They were talking about things that seemed important at the time, and then the afternoon was gone, and the white of the windows had turned wine yellow. Jason looked at her—his pupils grown enormous in the dark—and said, "What shall we do now that the museums are closed and Paris is blue?"

☾

When the girl gets home, several hours have passed. The politician has invited some friends over and her mother is setting the table for lunch. The girl finds wineglasses and cassis and starts making kirs. While she mixes them she watches the guests. There is a French film producer and his girlfriend, a woman so pretty and pale she looks like a cameo. There is another couple as well, a moon-faced Moroccan whose wife is from Brooklyn. Her long dark hair is suddenly white at the roots, as if age took her by surprise. The wife and the girl's mother, linked by ancient but profound New Yorkese, trade anecdotes on the theme of how rude the French are. Her mother tells the story of the man at the patisserie. The wife laughs with her mouth open, then says in sudden rage, "I'd like to give them a sock."

The girl lights a cigarette—her third—and as if this is a breaking point, Moroccan and wife, filmmaker and girl-friend, mother, all ask for cigarettes. She doles them out like candy.

"I've quit, really," says the girlfriend, her lean, soft face tilting up. "I buy packs and smoke one and leave the others in bars."

"They're awful," agrees the wife.

The girl says, "I'll quit by the time I'm twenty-five."

The politician snorts and explains, "She is obsessed with numbers. She will marry at thirty-eight, quit smoking at twenty-five. She assigns dates thus to her means of poison."

The girl looks at him and wonders if these statements of hers, which she had thought of as simply an attempt to be cute or clever, are in fact something serious: a need to restore order to the amorphousness of her life, to put boundaries up, to detach.

The conversation shifts to first marriages. All of them but the politician have had them, and there are more anec-dotes—the film producer's ex-wife stealing letters from his mailbox, his girlfriend's ex-husband calling her in the middle of the night to ask her where the television remote control was. They speak with some humor and some half-remote sadness. The girlfriend lifts her wineglass. "A toast to first love: Thank you, God, that it happens only once," and they all laugh.

☾

The girl is rinsing glasses in the kitchen, after the guests have left, when the phone rings. She picks it up, stumbling to say "*Âllo*," but it is her sister, Rose, who left Paris a week ago to live with her boyfriend in New York.

"Oh, it's awful," Rose says, her voice thin as water over long distance. "Eight restaurants have told me they won't hire college students as waitresses, because they leave them up in the air in August when they go back to school. They are so rude, too. They say it like they hate you."

"Eight?"

"Today Adrian and I had enough money to buy a hot dog. We cut it in half."

"Oh, Rosie. But you'll find a job," says the girl, asserting her oldest child's role of positive thinking.

"Well, it's more than that," says Rose, and for a second the girl thinks Rose is going to cry. "It's Adrian, too. We don't communicate anymore. The only thing we can communicate about is not being able to." The word "communicate" sounds strange and posed in her sister's mouth, a word she has learned from someone else. "I think I'll go to San Francisco, if Mom gives me the money for a ticket. I can see myself going nuts here, and saying crazy things in subways."

"Are you sure?" asks the girl. She has never met the boyfriend, and she is surprised by her sudden rage at him.

She thinks of sitting in the front hall telling her mother, "Remember you used to like him."

"We just don't like each other anymore," says Rose, and something in the heat of her voice makes the girl say, "Where is he now?"

"Lying on the bed."

"He's listening to this?"

"Sure."

The girl feels lightheaded and holds the telephone away from her. She is amazed at this method of communication—Rose is not talking to her, but to Adrian, bounced off the tinny-voiced backboard of The Sister. She remembers bickering with Jason before audiences, and she remembers letters she wrote to mutual friends, knowing Jason would see them: covert communication, always half hostile and half deprecating. She imagines Adrian lying facedown on Rose's bed listening to her say they don't like each other anymore: the intimacy of close stone throwing.

"Wait a minute; I'll get Mom," she says.

She walks into the living room to find her mother talking to the politician, their faces as close as lovers.

"Rose is on the phone," she says, and as her mother gets up quickly, the politician looks at the girl and smiles.

☾

In the morning the politician leaves, and her mother is sad. She cuts chanterelle mushrooms from the open market—the toughest mushrooms, she points out, but her heart is not in it—and she and the girl try to find lines of the politician's that they can crystallize into memories.

"When I moved to France he said I was institutionalizing my alienation," her mother offers.

"Here's one for the scrapbooks," says the girl. "He says that cynics are the greatest romantics of all, because they are the ones who have suffered for their ideologies."

That makes her mother laugh, and the girl is relieved that she will be able to keep private his final aside, which she thought over for a morning, smoking cigarettes as if smoke could blow it away: He had found her writing in her journal and said, "All that interests you is your self-referential lassitude."

❨

She is sitting on her bed playing solitaire. Enough days have passed that her mother has gone from talking about the politician constantly to talking about him often. Her mother, who smokes again, is holding a cigarette and not talking about the politician. She is telling the girl about a man she saw standing on a bridge over the Seine. He was holding open a large suitcase and throwing its contents into the water—women's clothes, a handbag, a pair of stockings. Her mother had been walking back from the Right Bank when she had seen this. She was quite far away and it had been difficult to tell, from his moving mouth and shoulders, whether the man was laughing or shouting.

"There are strange things in this world," says her mother.

The girl says, "Well, this is not nearly as good, but this morning I was walking by the Seine and I thought I saw Milan Kundera. He was sitting on a bench smoking, and he looked like the picture at the back of my book."

When the phone rings, her mother picks it up. Her face,

perplexed by these odd goings-on by the Seine, becomes suddenly tight. "It's for you," she says, holding out the phone, and in the sympathy of her voice the girl knows it is not Rose, asking for money.

At first she tries to negotiate with Jason. "Listen, I'm busy," she says. "I can't see you tomorrow. Let's see each other later, in school."

"Fine," he says. It is always a surprise to her to hear his voice on the phone; she cannot recreate it in her head. "That's great. Why don't you just walk into class in September. We can see each other then, in front of everyone."

"OK, OK," says the girl. "One-thirty tomorrow then," and there is no need to give him the building code, because he once lived in her mother's apartment with her for ten days. She tries to remember those days but three months seems a very long time ago, and stretches behind her like an arm pointing to something she can barely see.

☾

When he rings her doorbell at one-thirty, she is surprised. It is one of the facts that she has collected about Jason, in some file card registered in her brain, that he is always late, and she remembers being in England, angry that there was a party to go to and he was still in the shower. The past, with his exit from her life—another long-distance phone call—was rendered inviolable, exact. Now, in reentering, he has made everything subject to change, and she resents this petty violation of her code of order, of inevitabilities. She opens the door and he is standing there and again her perception of the past is rocked: His hair is shorter. He does not, to her eyes, look like himself, but then it is hard to remember how he looked. Her memories of him are oddly disembodied: She remembers his square fingertips, his eyes that turn yellow in some lights, the shape of his lips. Her pictures of him are all bad, and he is smiling in all of them, and now he is not smiling. She gets her cigarettes and they leave.

It begins raining immediately. The rain is as heavy and dense as a waterfall, and they go into a cafe. It is hard to look at him. Her head is too crowded with what she used to see.

She has played this scene too many times in her mind, and now that it is in motion, it is difficult to concentrate. She is amazed by her detachment. This, in her imagination, was going to be awful, but it is only bad. She must cut through many planes of her imagination and her anxiety to listen to what he is saying. It seems to her that she will only be able to hear him when he is gone.

Because they have abdicated the right to be nice to each other, and cruelty feels more intimate than indifference, they are deliberately, assertively unkind. But they had once been friends. There was a night she was in tears and he made her stand on her bed and dance with him. She smiles, and thinks that somewhere behind the ex-boyfriend persona that envelops him like a Japanese theatrical mask, there is Jason, and, possibly, if she tries hard enough, she will see him again. But it is hard to make herself try.

When Jason tries to take a picture of her, she catches his arm to push the camera away.

"I just want a photo," he says.

"What's the point?" she asks, and lights a cigarette to hide her face. Catching his arm alarms her. She thinks, I'm all right as long as I don't touch him.

They walk back by the Seine. The water has gone gray

and flat as stone, behind a bank of clouds that have blocked out the sun. This may make him remember a sunnier Paris, because he says, as she lights a dozenth cigarette, "What was that line again? 'What shall we do now that the museums are closed and Paris is blue?' Do you remember?"

"Yes."

"You were going to write me a story, with that as the title."

"I remember."

"Will you still write it?"

She thinks of poems he used to write and refuse to show her; he called her his anti-muse.

"Do I have to show it to you?" she asks.

"No."

"All right, I'll write it," she says, and looks at the river, trying to fix her eyes on something.

At some point when it seems impossible to imagine that they will ever get along again, she says, "Look, we'll have to see each other. We go to the same school, and we take the same classes."

"The same classes," he repeats, and she smiles at his expression.

"That's what you get for going out with an English major."

But later she finds it less easy to be flippant. They are walking on the street where her apartment is, and she pictures saying goodbye to him and watching him continue down the street. It seems to her that England would have been easier. Paris is too full of other things—kissing by monuments, steps on which they sat and drank wine. The ten days they spent in Paris was the time she was happiest with him, most in love, but suddenly those days seem trite to the point of being ridiculous. Once, when she and Jason were holding hands, walking through the Tuileries, a tourist took a picture of them. "We must look romantic," Jason said, and the girl had felt a rush of joy. Now, she hates to think that somewhere a woman has a photograph of her with Jason, smiling, holding his hand, smug in the non-reality of their love. She wonders how many couples have been conned by Paris into believing they are in love, only to leave their happiness behind them when they go. Jason asks, "What are you thinking?" and she says—she has reached a summit of not-niceness which is nearly ecstatic—"I wish we'd never come to Paris together."

She looks up at him and his face is stiff and set. All of a sudden memories of him which, while not at all erotic, are her best, crowd into her head: Jason stuffing her mailbox with mints, or chanting magic words over a cut on her knee, "So the hurt will go away to someone else's knee," all the silly, sweet things he had done and said and everything cast and overcast in friendship. She wants to touch him—not with remorse, but with concern: Who has done this to you? And she is taken aback that it is herself.

She spreads her hands. She wants to tell him things: Part of me has not stopped and will not stop caring about you. You were not just my lover, you were my best friend. She says what she can: "I'm sorry this is having a bad ending."

"No, you're not," he says. "That's just the way you wanted it."

When she was sulking on the Métro, Jason could make her laugh by saying, "You're such a martyr." Now, she smiles: caught. He is still mostly right about her. But he does not smile back, and after a moment she opens her apartment door and closes it behind her.

Her mother is sitting on the window seat needlepointing. In her lap the painted canvas with its patches of colored stitches looks like a stained glass window.

"How was it?" she asks.

The girl shakes her head. "Not so great."

She is poised for an *I told you so*—put of course in more maternal vocabulary—but her mother looks at her meditatively. "You know, I've been reading Proust's letters, and Proust says there's no such thing as a happy ending to a relationship, because it wouldn't end if it was happy."

Of course; that simple.

She goes into her bedroom and takes a spiral notebook from her shelf. She wants to start writing this story, quickly, so she can reduce Jason's new autonomy back into an abstraction. If she writes he is again past tense. He is a character in her story; she can choose which events and facets of a large story she will assemble to make a small one. He does not have to speak, and if he speaks, she can choose his lines from appropriate channels of her memory. She can control him again.

It can be a story about her, the continuation of her; he can be something dim and reconcilable in the past. Her friends accuse her of being obsessed with the past, but she sees herself as future-oriented as well; from the beginning of relationships, she looks towards the end. She had anticipated the breakup with Jason for so long that its actuality was familiar and comfortable. She is suddenly afraid that this will be the pattern of her life: Unhappiness will always be something that she understands better than happiness. She has been holding onto the fact that she is only twenty like an amulet: She is only twenty and much is left to happen to her. But she remembers realizing in her sophomore year that all of her essays, for all of her classes, had one basic theme—that love is pain—long before the theme was in any way justified by experience. Bitter without being embittered. Her mother, the politician, the woman toasting first love, Rose, Proust, herself, are all by their own arranging a colony of victims, resilient only in their anticipation of repeated failure.

But when she tries to write, memories of Jason keep slipping from her control. She thinks again of the night they danced on her bed. She had been fighting on the phone with her mother and Jason found her sitting on her bed crying. Jason sat by her, listening to her complain. All of a sudden, he said, "Come on, let's dance."

"What?" She looked at him, frowning. "Come off it."

But he was insistent, pulling her up by the armpits. "Stop pouting. Put your hand on my shoulder. Here. No, here. Didn't you ever take waltzing lessons?"

"Give me a break," she said. But she stood up. The mattress sank underneath her feet.

"Step back. Here, listen to me count. One, two—no, step back on one." Jason's hand was heavy and warm on her waist. "You really never took dancing classes? You're deprived. Turn around. Good! Now look up."

She lifted her head. He was looking down at her, laughing. "You're getting the hang of it."

Now and then, the girl would discover what she had known, in some compartment of her mind, for a long time. Dancing on her bed with Jason, she realized she was in love with him.

So why had she never told him? The words were easy enough. Once, he said, "If you loved me, you'd wash my socks," and, teasing, she told him, "Well, forget it then." Now she cannot shake that denial from her mind.

She had kept her feelings to herself, waiting. Testing him. "If you loved me, you'd give me a stamp for my letter," she told him, and Jason opened a drawer, took out a stamp, licked it, and rubbed it on the envelope—watching her eyes the whole time. Then. Why hadn't she told him then?

The time when it would have been an appropriate thing to say passed. At least that's what she told herself, logically, calmly. She was leaving, going back to California, and he was staying in England until the summer. They had to go on with their lives. It was silly to think about waiting for each other, to write vapid letters that said nothing, were full of kept secrets. Why complicate things.

Wincing, the girl remembers saying goodbye to Jason.

They were standing outside the Gare du Nord in Paris. Her arms were linked loosely around his neck. "What's going to happen to us?" he asked, and she kissed him to hush him.

"No point thinking about it now." She made her voice bright, clear. "Take care of yourself."

"You, too," he said, kissing her forehead.

Once her back was to him, once she had walked out of earshot, she let herself start crying. She felt as if all of the love she had kept contained was forcing itself through her eyes. Everything looked underwater. She was nearly at the end of the block, when she felt a hand pulling on her shoulder. She turned around. It was Jason.

"I wanted to say goodbye again."

"Why are you doing this?" she asked, humiliated. "Why are you making me unhappy?"

He hugged her. "We're both going to be unhappy alone soon. Can't we be unhappy together a little bit longer?"

That had been the end of it, the real end. The rest was just formal, clipping the strings.

The girl closes the notebook and leaves it on her bed. Oh Jason, she thinks, it's already too late to write you a story.

She picks up her keys and purse and walks out the door to buy cigarettes at the tabac on the corner. It faces the Seine, and from the street the water looks wide and slow-moving.

"Silk Cuts, *s'il vous plait*," she says.

The cashier is fat, with a face as soft and dense as dough. She pushes the package of cigarettes over the counter.

"*Merci*."

"*De rien*," the woman says, and turns away.

On the way home the girl tries to break down this phrase, "*de rien*." She has made a habit of trying to make sense of French—"*au revoir*" is "to see again." Linguistics never interested her in English; she never tries to puzzle the meaning of "good bye." But "*de rien*" confuses her: from nothing? Of nothing?

The rain has stopped, and the streets are damp and shiny, as if they have been polished. Paris looks clean to her, and light.

DRAGON

So we are sharing this bowl of noodles Finn likes, they're called dragon noodles, and out of nowhere he says, "Carla and I are getting back together." As if he's talking to some pure buddy, Jake or Donovan, not the girl he's been fucking for two months.

I freeze, fork halfway to my mouth. "What?"

He repeats it. He's twirling his fork in the bowl, twirl twirl twirl, not even looking at me.

A minute ago I was loose and comfortable. I didn't care if I had noodles sticking out of my mouth that I had to slurp, or sauce on my chin. I felt like a couple. Which is this campaign I've been on for the last couple of months, longer really: to hang in there without Finn noticing— "Oh, you're still here?" after everyone left once we'd watched that scary-as-shit movie in his basement, the air sweet from pot. It's been working. The other day his mother made me, not a meal exactly, but a plate of crackers with peanut butter on the side.

But now: I feel disgusting. I put down my fork and dab my chin, then look at the napkin. Nothing on it. I run my tongue over my front teeth. The dragon noodles have little black seeds, I think they are sesame seeds but have no clue why they are black, and I can feel them in the corners of my teeth like grit. I stand up, and Finn finally looks at me.

"I need to go to the bathroom," I say. There, I rinse my mouth and spit. I bare my teeth in the mirror. I don't see any seeds, but I can still feel them, grains of dirt. My eyes are wet.

In our high school there are three tiers with cement barricades between them. There are the kids like Finn and Carla who have their shit together and always did. Even back in grade school, you could tell from their school lunches: pita chips in Tupperware, green apples, thermoses of chicken soup. At the bottom are the burnouts. I am in the middle level, and it's the hardest climb. But I look up, and there's Finn, something to move toward. I imagined I could trick him into being truly mine. Looking in the mirror, I see the only idiot tricked here.

There's no fucking way I can go back to that table.

Thank God I never took off my sweater, and I have my bag with me, so what I do is walk straight out the back door. I'm half a block down the street before I have second thoughts. Finn will think I'm a freak; he's probably already wondering where I am. But if I go back I'll lose it. Then I register where I am, the overpass just ahead, and I know what will help.

Cooper is sitting on the sidewalk, legs extended. He's wearing his black shitkicker boots. He looks up when my shadow crosses him.

I say, "Hey," and he says, "Hey, yourself."

There's a stretchy pause. We haven't talked in months except nodding in the halls, but our conversation picks up where it broke off, because finally I say, "I need a hit."

He'd be a cute guy if his features weren't all bunched in the center, pulled tight by drawstrings. "Well, it ain't free," he says.

I look at the city rolling away from us.

"I don't have money," I say, which is true: I spent it on that stupid bowl of dragon noodles.

He extends his hand, and I pull him up. He's a heavy guy. We walk together under the overpass, being careful of nettles. He takes his crack pipe out of his pocket.

"Before or after?" he says.

I think about it, but I don't want to be high with my mouth full of cock, so I say, "After."

While he unzips his fly I kneel on the ground, checking for broken glass. He wraps his hand in my hair, almost tenderly, though it pulls, and I close my eyes. Here's the picture in my head: one of those orientation maps, like in the subway or a mall, with an orange dot that says, You are here.

FAMILY GAMES

Mel and Phil tell themselves they are doing this for the kids, that after weeks of tears and whisper-fights, normality is restored. Family game night is a way of staging "Look at how well Mom and Dad get along!" It's jazz hands.

The truth is more complicated. This truth is exposed when first Silas and then Cora retreat, yawning, to their respective bedrooms, Silas to his iPad, Cora to *A Wrinkle in Time*, and leave Mel and Phil by the fire, still duking it out.

This new game is a weird one. Phil bought it at a store called Marbles—"games for the brain." It's a bit like Chinese checkers, a bit like rubbing your stomach while patting your head. Mel can't quite get the hang of it, but the player tokens fascinate her. Such different sizes and shapes, they seem to have migrated from six entirely unrelated games. Phil's token, for instance, has octopus tentacles and is made of stretchy rubber. The thing has the wingspan of his forehead. Whereas Mel selected the smallest token, a spiky, mud-colored sphere the size of a gumdrop.

"What is this supposed to be?" Phil says, inspecting it.

"Prickly pear?" Mel speculates.

But privately she thinks it is a landmine, or a spiny rock-fish, lying in wait for an unsuspecting foot.

"Time for bed?" Phil says.

But now that bed means separate rooms—Phil sprawled

out, tentacles spread, on their California king, Mel whorled like a snail shell in the lumpy guest bed—neither of them is in any hurry to quit playing.

☾

They always liked games. Back in grad school, they first met at a get-to-know-each-other picnic for their cohort in Levy Park. The poets and fiction writers, all from elsewhere, were stunned and dopey in the Florida heat.

"Hydrate," second-years told them, handing out beers, water bottles, plastic cups of lemonade. "You'll get used to it."

Mel never did. The Florida sun always felt like a padded mallet bonking her on the head, whack-a-mole style. Perhaps she would have curled up in the shade with the moaning poets, had it not been for Phil, glossy with sweat, loud and stubborn.

"Hey, does anyone want to play badminton?"

He had brought a badminton set to Tallahassee when Mel had brought barely anything at all. When she had packed as if for a lifeboat, limiting her decorations to a few moody postcards, a blue ashtray from Caviar Kaspia.

"Sure, I'll play." She helped him shake out and extend the net.

☾

To excel at Scrabble, you must be able to anagram: live, evil, vile, veil.

For Pictionary, go for efficiency: the compact doodle. Don't get distracted getting the details right, perfecting the curl of an antenna.

For Clue, you need a system. Mel keeps track when everyone passes. Her Clue sheets are columns of initials: S, C, and P have all passed on the Revolver. Phil has an entirely different system, inscrutable to her. After games, she looks at his sheets and puzzles over what the annotations mean.

Always they stick with the classic versions. There is a new Clue that has incorporated unfamiliar weapons. Poison is one. A new Stratego reverses the power spectrum, so now the Marshall, instead of being #1, is #10. But #10 makes no sense—#1 is, intuitively, the most powerful. She and Phil shake their heads over this boneheaded revision. In stores, it's important to examine the boxes carefully. The most desirable Clue of all, though hard to find, has the Miss Scarlet she and Phil remember from their respective childhoods (Mel's in Fresno, California, Phil's in Des Moines): the one where Scarlet has dark, straight hair and hooded eyes and wields a cigarette holder.

☾

When they were graduate students, Mel and Phil played a game they invented called "Four-Letter Word Game."

"It's not what you think," they would tell their friends. Think of a four-letter word where all letters are different, no duplication. The other person guesses the letters. It was like Hangman, but you contained the data in your head.

Lying on the guest bed, Mel remembers one time when she finally had Phil's four letters nailed down. "Is the word wolf?"

"No."

"Flow?"

He was giddy with delight. "No!"

"Fowl!"

"On the third try!" He was crowing, so pleased. Their poet and fiction friends, at the same bar table, though long since disengaged from this bizarre Phil and Mel game, laughed, because Phil's glee was infectious. It is his great talent, pleasure.

Mel was skeptical. "I bet you were cheating. I bet it was wolf."

"I never cheat!" Phil said, shocked. Then he amended, making his Borscht Belt comedian face: "I mean, I never cheat at games."

☾

Mel knows Angie by sight from school drop-offs. Her hair, a fluffy nimbus, looks like a dandelion. Nonetheless, they have never been formally introduced. Mel feels like a seventh-grader, trying to ratchet up nerve to approach some intriguing girl. She makes herself extend her hand.

"Hi, I'm Mel Garrick. My kids are Cora in fifth grade and Silas in third."

Angie nods. "Oh, right. I know who you are. The writer's wife. You're married to Phillip Garrick, right?"

Mel flinches, which makes Angie wince. "Sorry! What a terrible thing to say."

"Well, actually," says Mel, "That's what I wanted to talk to you about."

☾

Another game, more compelling by far to Phil and Silas than to Mel or Cora: baseball. The boys sit in the stands watching the Giants, Silas marking his scorecard. K, Mel knows, stands for strikeout (knockout). Mel doesn't like baseball, but she understands its rules, this one in particular: three strikes and you are out.

The three strikes in this case:

Sharon, whom Mel thinks of as "the acolyte." Skin so pale she reminded Mel of a glass of bluish milk. She was one of Phil's students. When Mel pictures her, she imagines that scene in *Raiders of the Lost Ark* where a lecture room of enamored girls watch Indiana Jones teach. One has "Love you" written on her eyelids.

Strike Two is Anna Atkiss, a writer whom Mel has read but never met. Before Phil had an affair with Anna, Mel loved her novel. She recommended it to Phil. "Not really your style, babe, but so good." It had a starfish on the cover. When Phil met Anna at a conference, the first thing he said to her was, "My wife loves your book!" He told this to Mel on the phone that night, before he stopped talking about Anna, before Mel threw away her book.

Strike Three is Nadine.

☾

When Angie discovers the nature of what Mel wants to discuss, she upgrades their coffee plan to a drink. "Best canvassed over booze."

It turns out that Mel is not the first wife to seek her out. Angie explains this over Manhattans. She has become something of a local celebrity at their school, the poster girl of the amicable divorce. "I should hand out business cards," Angie says grimly, shaking the ice in her glass.

She tells Mel her story. Her husband fell in love with

an associate at his firm. The thing that Angie finds retro-spectively annoying is that she liked this woman. Well, she liked Martha's boyfriend more. They had the couple over for dinner, several times.

"I actually wondered what the boyfriend, a dynamic, inter-esting guy, was doing with Martha. She seemed a little drab."

"She wasn't attractive?"

"Well. She has big eyes, short hair. She looks like an extra-terrestrial. She's attractive, I suppose, the way an extrater-restrial is attractive."

Mel laughs so hard she spits out a mouthful of Manhattan. This is the moment she knows she and Angie will be friends. Years from now, she might elbow Angie and say, "That woman over there is attractive the way an extraterrestrial is attractive."

But this forecast also makes Mel's eyes tear. Because it used to be Phil that she would have these private, silly jokes with, not some stranger-friend who looks a little startled, then laughs.

Angie continues. Even though she clicked more with Stephen, the boyfriend, she considered Martha a friend. So when Angie found out about the affair, her initial reaction was rage. She talked to herself in the shower. Though she often addressed these monologues to her husband Bob, just as frequently she berated Martha.

"How could you?" Angie says. "That's what I kept saying to invisible phantom Martha. How could you?" She sighs. "So I don't mean this to sound all fluffy and Zen, because fuck that. But here's what I realized: Hatred corrodes the vessel." She shrugs. "I know! I sound like a fortune cookie. But all this bitterness I contained, all this vitriol, was torqueing me into a sour, injured person. Of course it was also terrible for our kids. So I 'womaned up,' is the verb I use. Because let's face it, men have no capacity to do this shit. Even though Bob was squarely in the wrong, it took me saying, 'OK, enough already, olive branch,' for us to normalize things. Only then could he stop being an asshole about money, because you know lawyers, the stinginess is structural. Only then could we make things less toxic for the kids."

Amicably divorced women are safe to admire, is Angie's theory, because it involves no envy. Everyone admired Mother Teresa, since no one wanted to be her.

"So tell me," Angie says. "What's it like to be married to a famous writer?"

"Barely married. Unmarrying."

☾

Now they call it uncouples therapy. Dr. Beckman has been with them for the haul, since strike one. They have graduated and then slunk back to him more than once; "We're recidivists," Mel and Phil say.

But ever since Mel's revelation that there is no getting over Nadine, that she simply cannot forgive (pretend to forgive) and forget (pretend to forget) one more time, it has been uncouples therapy. As such, it has ceased to be the Phil Garrick show, their status quo, even back in grad school when Phil was merely glittery with potential, but exponentially more so since his prizes. Even a venue that is structurally geared towards balance, like couples therapy, has historically been Phil's show.

But now Mel directs the program. Ever since her announcement, "I don't want to be married anymore, but I want to do this right."

Civil. Kind. Supportive. But no awful, phony, Gwyneth Paltrowesque "conscious uncoupling" shit.

Dr. Beckman praises Mel's candor and generosity. But Mel gets Angie's point about the admiration, about what makes Mel palatable: There is nothing to envy about her situation.

☾

San Francisco has become insane. At night, Phil snoring away in the giant king bed like the giant king he is, Mel looks through Craigslist and panics. She will need at the very least a two-bedroom for the kids—assuming she can force Cora and Silas to share a room. Phil likes to say Cora and Silas get along about as well as Republicans and Democrats in Congress. To this, the kids respond, like the Blue State children they are, "I don't want to be the Republicans!" So Phil designates Republicanism as a penalty: "Last one to the car is the Republicans!"

Crappy two-bedrooms in the Mission are going for five grand. She should have left Phil in 2008, after the real estate crash, after Strike One. Mel refreshes and refreshes, as if a new search will scrub away this Googlification of San Francisco.

Phil's position with the house is like his stance on the master bedroom: She is very welcome to come back, he always says, when she complains about not sleeping well in the lumpy guest bed. This is her choice, not his. One morning, watching her sigh over Craigslist, he points to the twelve-by-nine shed in the back yard.

"You could live there!"

Mel stares at him. He is obviously being serious, though when he absorbs her expression, he tries to rearrange his face to convey, instead, joking.

"Phil," she says. "I am not a dog."

"I was thinking of you more like a garden hose. Or a rake."

"Dude," she says, "You are the rake."

Sometimes Mel thinks Phil hands her these lines, like they used to set up each other's stories.

"You tell the next part."

Stories for Mel and Phil, at least the good stories, were community property, something to refine collaboratively. They were a relay team. But the downside of being a couple who composes stories is that the story supersedes the lived experience. At age thirty-nine, with Phil now for fifteen years, Mel remembers not so much how they met as the retold story of how they met: unfurling the badminton net together like a scroll, trying to rally the faint, sun-stunned poets and writers: "Come and play!"

Then, no one would play with Phil except Mel. Now, there's a line of volunteers.

☾

Mel once read a Facebook thread where a writer friend, a guy from their MFA program, posed this question: "Writers: When did you start identifying to strangers as a writer, instead of as whatever job actually pays your bills?"

The thread, by the time Mel came across it, was already a mile long. The upshot was that most writers did not (though, as more than one pointed out, of course they all privately considered themselves writers. Why else were they responding to Dave's address to "writers"?). Officially, though, most introduced themselves as teachers, editors, sommeliers. Very few writers were in Phil's position, with his prizes, his bestsellers, his tenure at Stanford.

Yet what stunned Mel about this thread was that she always identified as a writer, even though she hasn't written anything in six or seven years. Anything, that is, but checks, and notes Silas demands for his lunchbox ("I'm so proud of you! Love you, Mom"). She's like a fat person who doesn't consider herself fat. While ninety percent of writers might suffer from crippling insecurity, she has historically been so confident that it shocks her to realize she is thirty-nine, virtually unpublished, and her husband keeps cheating on her. That even though she always thought they were a perfectly matched team, they are in fact on opposing sides, and she has lost this game.

☾

Back in grad school, they called themselves Philomel: the woman in Greek myth who was raped by her brother-in-law Tereus. He cut out her tongue to keep her from telling on him. Stupid man to assume that communication could only happen vocally! Maimed Philomel wove her story into a tapestry for her sister, and the two sisters took revenge by killing his son and feeding him to Tereus. Afterwards, Philomel transformed into a nightingale, communicating through song instead of speech.

"That is a fucking creepy domain name," said their friend Dave, the same Dave of the Facebook query, when they told him the story. They took turns: Mel told the rape part, Phil the cannibal part.

☾

More about names: Mel never liked her given name Melanie (too cheerleader-ish), and as an eight-year-old chose Mel as both nickname and penname. Mel was jaunty; Mel was abbreviation for "mellow," "mellifluous." Now it seems to stand for grimmer things: melancholy, melanoma. She considers readopting Melanie, in the same way she considers other transformations (dying her hair dark blue, shaving her head).

Phil's name connotes plenitude. It lends itself to dirty jokes, sex talk ("Phil me," Mel used to say in bed). He had never much liked Phillip ("Fillip: It's a snap; it's a finger-flick"). And yet, for years, for his entire publishing life, he has been Phillip Garrick. People say, "Oh, you're the wife of Phillip Garrick!" and stare at Mel, as if she can tell them secrets.

She hears him, these days, introduce himself as "Phillip Garrick," both names. She wonders, like the caterpillar with the hookah in the Alice story, Who are you?

☾

Another family game night, the kids long since gone to bed, Phil drops his token with the rubbery tentacles down Mel's shirt. She shrieks.

(Mel wonders what one's selection of a particular board game avatar says about a person. What does it mean that in Monopoly, Phil is the elongated car, while she is the thimble? What does that finger-armor signify?)

Watching Mel pluck the octopus from its clutch onto her bra, Phil laughs. When she extracts it and looks up, his face becomes more solemn.

"Is it OK to say?" he says. "I mean, to say I love you?"

"Not after five o'clock," says Mel. "It's the reverse of cocktail time. No declarations of affection after five."

❪

Their neighbors in the family housing complex in Tallahassee were a pair of PhD students in English literature, who got into screaming fights about Hegel. Mel and Phil would lie in bed and listen to them through the cardboard walls.

"I am not your Foucault warden!" shouted Ethel, the woman. "Don't stick me in your fucking panopticon!"

I am not your Foucault warden.

She's attractive the way an extraterrestrial is attractive.

These scraps float in Mel's brain. She curates; she discards one, inserts one. She has never been good about clearing debris. If you haven't worn it in the last year, send it to Goodwill. But Mel can always imagine a situation in the future where she might wear that striped jumpsuit. This is why she used to fail the written portion of her driver's test: She treated the multiple-choice questions as tricks. She thought of circumstances (walls of opaque fog) that might require that otherwise counterintuitive answer C.

But she is trying to get better about this, to treat letting go as a skill to develop.

❪

Even their wedding was a game. They threw a Halloween costume party the second year in Tallahassee, and dressed as a bride and groom. Well, vampire-victim bride and ghoul-groom: on Mel's neck, she painted puncture wounds, exuding a perfect teardrop of blood.

Towards midnight, Phil clinked a fork to his glass, and they rounded up their guests for a surprise ceremony. Only their officiant, Eliza, knew in advance.

Phil always tells the punchline of this story: "We were married by a gumball machine."

☾

Mel rubs her neck. "So tired. I hate that fucking bed."

"You can always come back," Phil says.

She wonders. Her resolve (three strikes and you're out) has allowed Phil to claim his position: He wants to make things work. His door is literally open. This is the story he presents in uncouples therapy.

Sometimes Mel looks at Dr. Beckman and imagines herself as the star student, the one who shines, as she never shone in the MFA program (that was Phil). Though in her heart she knows, if Dr. Beckman brags about them to his wife, if he insinuates when he sees someone reading a particular book that he knows the author, that the star is Phillip Garrick.

Still, Beckman approves of Mel: her compassion, her humor about the bleak rental market. The rake in the garden shed story made him laugh: She and Phil are still performing their relay routine.

And Phil approves, too. Mel has become, once again, the game girl he met fifteen years ago, with the tattoo of the fly on her collarbone.

How would either man react to some dissolve of will? To Mel in retreat?

It's a risk, and Risk is the one board game Mel hates (exhausting, the pounding of soldiers onto soldiers, the unthrilling goal of world domination).

If she says, "OK, you're on," what then?

Would she call Phil's bluff? Force him to concede that the open door is only rhetoric. He doesn't really want her back after all; he's already casting his eyes down the line of volunteers, the starry girls with "Love you" painted on their eyelids?

Celebrities like to trumpet the value of old friends, the people who knew them when and before. These are the people they really trust, celebrities say, because their love is authentic. These love the "real" person, not the construct.

But the obverse of knowing someone before fame is that the unfamous identity is always part of the composite picture. Mel knew Phil when he was a sweaty grad student with a unibrow, trying unsuccessfully to rally poets to play.

His first book, after the title page, reads, "To my Mel, this dedication for her dedication." At age thirty, Mel loved the double play: It seemed to forecast her own book in the future, to take it for granted. She could see her novel's spectral outline, calling back to him.

If she says "Honey, I'm home," or "OK, you win," might he say, as their kids do, as she herself when a kid did, "No backsies"? Would his mask finally drop? And if it did, would Mel feel, at last, actually free? No longer on her thirty feet of bungee cord, tethered to the California king. She imagines she would stretch her nightingale wings, open her non-uttering but still vocalizing throat. She might, like Philomel, kick-start her flight away.

HOW TO FALL OUT

Lack the technology skills to change your Facebook settings so you can block posts you don't want to see. Plus, fear drastic moves, like unfriending: anything detectable, anything that might raise questions.

Combine this with the voyeurism that leads you to scan the crumpled car for injured bodies, or that makes you stand in front of your mirror, pinching that rubbery roll of fat, examining that parabolic scar, like someone stapled your cheek, right there.

Consequently, be assaulted by status updates from his wife: "Enjoying date night with my Robert." "Lighting candles to eat dinner with my sweetheart." "Celebrating twenty years with my beloved Robert."

To this last, do not click "Like"; "Like" is beyond you, beyond anyone sane. But scan, nonetheless, the scroll of comments ("Congratulations!" "Much love to the best couple ever!"). Locate his comment in that endless, endless string: "May there be twenty more! Love you."

Try to read something meaningful into that "Love you," into the fact that the "I" is excised, the subject erased. Is this a covert nod, an indicator that he is not really present in this declaration? Could Descartes possibly say, "Think, therefore am," and have the meaning hold? Contemplate this for a day.

Then give up on that shit.

☽

Spot him, later that week, sitting at a table talking to Mahsa, your new colleague. Study Mahsa's straight back, her ribbed, olive turtleneck, her ringletty hair that makes you think of coiled springs. See him lean forward on his elbows. Recognize, in the tilt of Robert's head, his lop-sided smile, how, a year ago, he looked at you. You are too far away to hear what they are saying, but when it comes to such detections, you have X-ray vision. You are Superman, and you wish your eyes, like his, could emit laser beams.

☽

Now, listen to yourself. Listen when you tell your students to pay attention to the rhetoric we have for love. Hear yourself say desire, from the Latin verb *desidare*, means "to wish, to long for." Point out to your students the implications of that: desire gropes toward what it can't quite touch. Once sated, it ceases to mean, to be, desire.

They laugh, they groan. (It's this kind of talk that has given you a certain pedagogical reputation. You are the Ghost of Christmas Future; you say weird shit. One class wanted to get you a coffee mug inscribed, "You're all going to die.") But this time, actually process your spiel, the litany you tick off for them: *crush, captivate, mad about, crazy about, head over heels, intoxicate.* All those words represent love as coercion, lunacy, poison.

"Why do we fall in love, rather than rise in it?" Hear yourself pose the question. Actually straighten up, in that basement lecture room with its tiered seating and cavelike acoustics. Your students are doing their laughing, groaning thing, but you concentrate on some elusive echo.

Picture yourself at the bottom of something dark and damp; look up at the circle of light. Like a mime, extend your palm. Realize the wall is laddered with rungs you can grip. They might be smooth as a faucet, or they might be rubbery, like the handles of your bike. Whatever works.

Take hold of one. Now climb up and out of this rabbit hole.

CHIN CHIN CHIN

I know exactly how Shoulda is going to react, so I wait a couple of days to call and ask if I can bring a "plus one" to her Christmas party.

She groans. "Oh, don't tell me!"

I agree not to tell her.

"It's the LUG, isn't it? The fucking LUG. Every holiday season: She's like the eternal return. Egg nog, reindeer sweaters, and the LUG."

I only half listen. I'm occupied watching the LUG, whose real name is Penelope, walk across my kitchen to get a glass of water. She's wearing my San Francisco Giants tank top, no bra, and a pair of green panties, and damn, is Penny fetching. Her ass, as she presses her glass to the water dispenser, is a rind of watermelon.

So I barely hear Shoulda say, "Nat, you know she'll be gone as soon as New Year's Eve is over. Back to the land of men, blowing you a kiss over her shoulder. She just can't stand to be alone for the holidays. She's like a stray cat you keep feeding saucers of milk to."

"So can I bring her?" I say.

Shoulda sighs. "Fine, you pathetic sucker, but you better bring something decent to drink, if my party is getting besmirched by that goddamned LUG."

Later, we're watching *Bladerunner*, or rather Penny is

watching it, while I watch her lick salt from her fingertips. Penny says, "Your friends don't like me."

And what can I say? It's true. Even in college, when Penny was my girlfriend for a semester and spent most nights in my twin bed and wore my clothes, helped herself to all my earthly possessions—my expensive conditioner, my bomber jacket—even then; my friends were leery, Shoulda most of all. My friends had nomenclature for sexual orientation, just like we did for everything: straight, wavy, and curly. "At best," Shoulda said, of Penny, "She's wavy."

And sure enough, as soon as Penny cross-listed a class at Berkeley where there were actual men to borrow lecture notes from, I got chucked to the wayside. Though between boyfriends, when she was stoned or lonely, Penny ended up in my bed often enough to fire up my hopes that perhaps she'd stay.

Eight years later, it's like Shoulda said: She reappears during the holidays, when she can't stand being alone, when whatever shellac and chipper smile Penny wears to be that Merry Single Girl crumbles to paint chips. In January, she's gone again, as if being straight is the first of her New Year's resolutions. Though she'll leave me a present when she goes: soapstone, a charm for my bracelet, or once, a doll with a head made of a dried apple: Under its checkered bonnet peers a wizened, brown face.

I put the doll in my bar cabinet; I looped its blue, gingham arm around the neck of a Grand Marnier bottle. "That doll is creepy as shit," Shoulda says, when she comes over.

"She must be great in bed," Shoulda surmised once, wistfully, and I nodded, because—why? Because I'm defensive? Or gallant? The truth is, Penny lies back and lets me do all the work. But hard to call it work: the sticky feel of her on my tongue.

Do I care that she will leave me in January? I ask myself, watching her lick popcorn salt from her fingers. That she will leave behind some dumb memento, some paperweight, some corkscrew shaped like a cockatoo?

Maybe it's being jaded and old, I turn twenty-eight in two weeks, but I don't give a shit. I think of a Townes Van Zandt song Shoulda plays for me: "You wear your skin like iron." I feel as dry and tough as that apple doll.

There was a time when Penny made me cry. Now I lie in bed and watch her get dressed to work out. I watch her pull on her leggings, hitch on her sports bra, and I think, "I am sleeping with a girl who wears lipstick to the gym." Every word in that sentence feels foreign to me, a thought bubble that belongs to some other schmuck: not just the obvious absurdity of wearing lipstick to the gym, like some dot-com slave who lives in the Marina, who goes to pubs with flat-screen TVs, who jogs with her boyfriend along the picture postcard Crissy Field, the Golden Gate Bridge strutting in the background, but also the words "girl" (Penny is twenty-seven), and "sleeping."

Though what verb applies to our activities? Can I really call the way Penny lies back and spreads her legs "fucking" her?

She's like a cat who closes her eyes and purrs.

Hours later, I watch her shimmy into a sleeveless pink dress. That dress makes me think of those rectangular erasers with the soft corners I used to carry in my vinyl pencil bag. And even though that memory belongs to middle school, and not college, where I first met Penny (Intro to Women's Studies), where I first spread her out on my lumpy twin bed, I am hit with a wave of nostalgia: the fruity smell of Penny's hair; her husky voice, asking to borrow my notes. Sitting next to me later at Founder's, Shoulda checking her out, Shoulda's eyes already squinting.

There's no love lost between Penny and Shoulda, though Penny lumps all my friends together. Penny purses her lips and says, "Your friends are," and you can pick your adjective to fill in that Madlib, but only from the barrel of negative adjectives: "elitist," "bitter," "pretentious," "mean."

But when we get to Shoulda's party, they are both all smiles. Shoulda opens the door. Her eyes move down Penny's dress, and she says, "You look gorgeous, Penny!" Penny beams, because that girl feeds on compliments. They are the fingers that knead her fur.

"Oh, you do, too, Shoulda," she says, though I can tell that Penny doesn't mean it: that she's looking at Shoulda in her blue vintage dress with the puffy crinoline skirt and tight waist, and thinking she looks fat.

I like the way Shoulda looks, though: like she dissected a music box.

We walk in, and whoa, the place is fancy. Not Shoulda's miniscule studio in the Excelsior, but a giant two-story upper flat in Noe Valley. Through the bay window, San Francisco unfurls: In the distance I can see the strung beads of the lighted Bay Bridge. This condo belongs to Bernice, Shoulda's girlfriend, who approaches. Bernice gives me a hug, eyes Penny, and drawls, "And who, sweetheart, are you?"

Bernice has only been around since summer, so she missed Penny's last holiday cycle through my life.

"Penny," Penny purrs.

That lascivious crone offers to get her a drink. She says, "Stella, darling, you're falling down on your hostess duties."

Shoulda rolls her eyes, as Bernice carts Penny away.

"Without even asking, please note, whether I might like a

drink," I point out to Shoulda, who shrugs. "And what the fuck: She calls you Stella?"

Another shrug. "Well, that is my name."

I feel forlorn. Is this what it is like to be forgotten? Any marks I left water-writing, evaporating on the face of a rock? I am the Namer. In that capacity of the one who bequeaths adhesive names, I named Shoulda nine years ago. A bunch of us in my dorm lounged in the corridor, passing around my aluminum flask, and I christened her. She is Shoulda, because her name is Stella, but should have (shoulda) been Blanche: the melodramatic mess of a sister in *A Streetcar Named Desire*, instead of the intimidated, married one. And why Shoulda, instead of Blanche? Because therein lies the genius of naming: the unpredictable left turn, the spitball.

Shoulda loops her arm around my shoulder, and says, "To you, Nat, I will always be Shoulda. Now let's get you something brown."

She walks me, not to the bar draped with a red cloth where Bernice is leering at Penny, but to the kitchen. It's shiny as a spaceship. From a cabinet Shoulda pulls out bourbon and two glasses.

Am I the Namer, anyway? Suddenly I'm doubting myself. Did I not, after all, try to stamp something sexier, something befitting of a royal mistress, onto Penny, only to be shut down in my attempt to rename her Nell? Penny clutched onto the flat, copper disc of her name with the same stubborn resolve with which she resists my every effort to remake her.

And to Shoulda and the rest of my friends, Penny is and will always be LUG: the lesbian-until-graduation, or in recent years, until New Year's Day.

We both take big swallows of our bourbon, which I see is some expensive brand: Four Roses.

"Chin chin," Shoulda says.

I say what I always say back to her, "Chin chin chin." Because that woman has a jaw like Jay Leno, she is Shoulda-of-the-lantern-jaw. Two chins is simply not enough.

She laughs, a little dourly, and I study her strange face, flat like a bulldog's, but with that long, broad chin. Her hair is dyed the color of red velvet cake. We had sex once, when we were twenty-three, both of us high on ex. I remember licking the center of Shoulda's moist palm, and that ecstasy feeling of having to puke.

"I need to stop drinking this stuff," says Shoulda, contemplating her glass.

Though this is hardly the first time Shoulda has made such a declaration, there is a resolve in her tone that makes me say, "Why?"

"We're thinking about getting pregnant."

Again, every word in that sentence seems foreign. I hate it when couples talk about "we" getting pregnant, like they are conjoined, wielding a shared uterus. Somehow it's even worse when it's two women. But pregnant, with Moneybags? With that crone, who at this very moment is ogling Penny's boobs, sculpted into missiles by Penny's retro bra?

In that uncanny thermometer way she can gauge every dip and spike in my mood, Shoulda says, "What's wrong?"

I shift from Penny's pointy breasts to a panning shot of her whole manifestation. For a moment that eraser dress seems to function, *Fantasia* style, like an animated eraser, sweeping away all dregs of Penny's abandonments: the apple doll, the charm shaped like a referee's whistle. Then the dress erases Penny altogether.

I turn to look at Shoulda, who despite her squashed face and giant chin, has beautiful, light green eyes: the distilled color of Pernod. I remember, six or seven years ago, sitting with Shoulda at some bar in the Boulevard de Montparnasse, clinking our glasses of cloudy green Pernod, and saying, "Chin chin chin."

It's a Four Roses revelation. "Shoulda, I should be with you," I say.

Her mouth is a wry pucker; she's about to say something disparaging. But then she seems to realize I speak without, for once, that dollop of irony that we serve on every last thing we say to each other: like too much frosting on a cupcake.

Because she smiles; her Pernod eyes sparkle. She says, "Well, it took you long enough to figure that out."

SORRIED

Sitting on the back deck, Daniel cracks open a pilsner with the crappy can opener that he keeps forgetting to replace. He looks through the glass sliding doors at his wife, whom he loves, who is cheating on him.

Beth sits cross-legged on the living room floor, playing Sorry! with their three-year-old, Olivia. Several feet from them, his back to the wall, their son Gideon pages through *The Little Engine That Could*. Gideon will not play games, or, more precisely, no one, not even Beth, will play games with Gideon. Any time a piece of his gets sent home, he wails; his face folds into a fist. "Oldest child," is Beth's diagnosis, which Daniel (oldest child himself) takes personally: There go Beth and Olivia, calm and unruffled, while he and Gideon, the orchids, wilt and brood.

Beth looks up and smiles, a wry shrug of a smile. Daniel nods, but cannot bring himself to return it.

What to do, what to do. The words cycle through his brain, a paralyzed version of that book Gideon has on his lap, about the determined little engine who chugs up the mountain, chanting "I think I can, I think I can." It amuses Beth that this book drives Daniel batshit, though she worries about Daniel's "bleakness." Beth insisted he start seeing a shrink nine months ago.

"Shrink": it's a noun Daniel takes literally. He imagines Beth trying, through elegant Anita Kopchik, to make Daniel's moroseness smaller, manageable, something that can be folded into one of their cabinets with the nickel-plated knobs.

Through the glass, he watches Beth throw up her hands in mock despair as Olivia Sorries her, gleefully bonking Beth's yellow plastic piece with the butt of her blue one, pinching it between her small fingers and twirling it home.

Beth's nickname sounds like a caress: *Beth*, as soft as socks. Her blond hair (dyed), her silky throat (circled with a thin gold chain, a Mother's Day present, through which Beth strings different pendants, Olivia's crescent moon, Gideon's acorn): Everything about Beth soothes.

Daniel has known about Beth's affair for nearly thirty-six hours. That's how long he has known-known. Days ago suspicion felt as intolerable as an itch.

So far, only one-and-a-half other people know: his best friend Teddy is the half, his therapist Anita the whole. Two nights ago, over beer at their local, Teddy agreed that Beth's behavior of late was "pretty fucking suspicious." Really, this is why Daniel told him about Beth's dreaminess, about the panicky way she closed her laptop; he needed someone to grant him permission to read Beth's email ("Well, *I* fucking would").

Anita took it in stride, steepling her beautiful fingers. (In their sessions Daniel finds himself transfixed by those fingers). "So what do you want to do, Daniel?"

To do to do to do. Run together, it sounds like what his British mother would exclaim in her kettle-whistle pitch: "What a todo!"

There are plenty of tasks Daniel does for the pool-playing adolescents with whom he works, "the kids," he calls his dot-com colleagues, in their expensive jeans. But the most relevant part of his job is risk assessment. Sometimes, Daniel conceptualizes the green, rolling hills of a golf course, studded with sand traps.

A course of action is what Daniel needs. "Course" makes him think of navigable routes. This can be survived; Daniel will not simply lose Beth, his Beth of ten years. Beth from whom he would check out library books (Daniel a graduate student, Beth an undergrad whose work-study was at the reference desk) until he could ratchet up the nerve to speak to her—who would smile at him after she stamped each unnecessary book.

He pictures shaking her emails at her, the stack he printed. He pictures Beth begging him to forgive her while he looks coldly into her wet, blue eyes.

Then the image pops. The golf course becomes overwhelmed by sand traps, a desert. He winces at the whiplash of grit.

What if he confronts her and her face becomes red and blotchy? If she says, "Fuck you, you hypocrite"? (Yesterday, Anita made this point more diplomatically: "Does this make you think about Lecia?") Or if, instead of getting angry or defensive, she says, simply, "I love him"?

Words singe Daniel: *no fault state, alimony, custody.*

Can he do nothing at all? Already, in this last thirty-six hours, Daniel is avoiding Teddy's texts: "You OK?" and then "Well?" and then, simply, "???" Is it possible to avoid Teddy for the rest of his life?

To avoid his own burnt-black memory? To kiss his wife? To fuck her, like he did last night, from behind, holding her hips, so he didn't have to look into her eyes? So he could feel only the heat and grip of her? Can he become the little engine that could, can he will himself to carry dolls, stuffed bears, bags of peppermints, and dimply oranges up that mountain?

POP GOES THE WEASEL

One by one, Nina's friends from her moms' group have gone back to work. It's a march Nina watches with chagrin, since the most interesting mothers bail first. Raunchy Iris started working part-time, but switched to full-time after telling Nina that her days at the bank felt like her days off.

"I just don't have a twenty-four/seven stay-at-home mom in me!" is the consensus.

At the reunion party in May when the ten babies (all spring birthdays) are a year old, Nina and Becky are the only holdouts still not working. Nina would gladly trade Becky for any of the other moms. Officious Becky makes her own baby food, jamming roasted yams through a potato ricer and freezing the puree in ice cube trays. Becky corrals Nina into exchanges ("I'll make yams tomorrow, and you do mashed asparagus").

At the reunion picnic, holding Jonah between her knees, Nina describes the aftermath of one of these baby food exchanges to Iris. Nina's husband Nathan, making cocktails, assumed the zipper-sealed bag of green ice cubes was some gourmet experiment of Nina's—cilantro or mint-infused ice—and squalled when informed that he had just put frozen mashed peas into his gin-and-tonic.

"Like with all my free time, I'd make specialty ice cubes," Nina tells Iris. "Who am I, Martha Stewart?"

Iris laughs, though her eyebrows raise. Their angle conveys that, unlike the working moms sprawling around them on Guatemalan blankets, Nina does indeed have free time.

There's a big dollop of boring involved in being a stay-at-home mom. There are long hours of kneeling in playgrounds, on that rubbery surface that seems to have replaced, within the parameters of Portland, Oregon, all the playground concrete, that makes Nina feel like she is perching on a deflated ball. No matter how many showers she takes, Nina's hair is always full of sand. There are moments when Nina longs to work, when she calls Manuel, her business partner (they are event planners, a team for the five years prior to Jonah's birth). She says, "I miss you. Talk grownup to me."

But in general, Nina enjoys pushing Jonah's stroller for miles in quest of *pain au chocolat*. She likes having nothing more pressing to do when Jonah naps than to gluestick photos into his scrapbook. The repetitive tasks sedate her: folding laundry, stenciling stars and crescent moons along the baseboard of the nursery. Nina has felt no sustained urge to follow the lemmings back to work.

Until her stepdaughter Laurel comes to stay for the month of June, and lands, like a cat with claws, in Nina's lap.

☾

Laurel has of course always been a factor, but primarily she's an abstraction.

When Nina met Nathan, he was married. As a favor for her college suitemate Cathy O'Neill, Nina planned the party for Cathy's thirtieth birthday. So four years ago, she flew to the Bay Area for the weekend: Berkeley where Nathan lived, the party in the Brazilian Room that he attended (he and Cathy worked in the same architecture firm). Nathan immediately caught Nina's eye. In his orange linen shirt, he reminded Nina of Buenos Aires, of the way her father and her uncles dress.

"They look like hibiscus flowers," she explained to Nathan, over champagne.

Nathan seemed both flattered and concerned that he was being mocked. "Don't know if I was aiming for hibiscus."

Later Nina learned his wife Alice had dressed him— "Wear that shirt I got you in New York"— before deciding, typical Alice, that she was seeing silver sparks, a migraine must be coming on, so she couldn't attend Cathy's party.

In those heady days of falling in love with Nathan, his daughter Laurel gave Nina pause, more than his wife.

Alice was easy for Nina to rationalize: self-absorbed Alice, too preoccupied with her artwork to pay attention to her husband; in the aftermath of their divorce, too crazy and weird to waste guilt upon. Nina liberated Nathan from an untenable situation.

Laurel is trickier, then and now. It's one thing to fall in love with an unhappily married man, itching for rescue; it's another to fall for the father of a ten-year-old. It seemed officially *wrong*; it seemed moreover like a pain in the ass.

As her partner Manuel put it, "There are plenty of unencumbered men out there." Why saddle herself, at thirty, to inconvenience?

It's hard for Nina to explain what makes Nathan worth the hassle. He is smart but not brilliant. He is good in bed but not extraordinary; she's had better lovers. She wonders how much of the draw stemmed from her initial impression: across the redwood-paneled room, his orange shirt.

Despite the fact that Nathan grew up in Denver and is solidly American, he reminds Nina of her father, of her uncles, of a particular way all three of those men, four if she folds in Nathan, chase pleasure. There is something irresistible about Nathan's enjoyment of things: a *tarte tatin* Nina dressed with fresh whipped cream; Nina's naked body. Even silly things, like the way he raves about Nina's lemon-grass shower gel: "This is the best thing I've ever smelled!" His capacity for pleasure disarms.

The downside of this, Nina is discovering, is that Nathan has limited tolerance for distress.

She thinks of him as a "tickle daddy." He's the kind of father who attacks his child right before bed, tickling the kid into hysterics, and then hands him to the mom. He isn't the twenty-first century, sling-wearing father most of the moms in her group married. When Iris's son Ricky defecates, Iris hands him to her husband. Nina can tell that Iris thinks it's strange (those raised eyebrows, again) that Nina is always the one who changes diapers.

Nina can only return to the orange shirt: We marry what is familiar.

To Nina, fathers were not present and responsible, but they were fun. They swooped in when one's mother was broke and pissed off, and they carted one to Patagonia for Christmas. They had a string of blade-thin girlfriends, they gave one opal earrings for Christmas, and they were, like the red and gold sparks in those opals, bright and flashy.

No doubt it's the half-Argentinian in Nina who makes her proud she "gave" Nathan a son, like some old-time British queen, though of course logically she knows it's the X or Y sperm that determines the infant's gender. Still, when Jonah was born, Nina felt that she scored. Take that, Alice the narcissist!

Now, Nina wants a daughter. Girls' clothes are prettier, and there are so many more appealing options for names. She broached the subject of a second baby with Nathan: "I don't want Jonah to be an only child."

Which for once made his eyebrows lift. "What about Laurel?"

More proof that Laurel, until this summer, has always been an abstraction.

When Nina first met her, Laurel was nearly eleven, almost as easy to win over as Nathan. Nina took her to a store in Russian Hill where they sampled candy displayed in glass jars. Afterwards, she sent a care package of Laurel's favorites to her summer camp (Swedish fish, chocolate-covered strawberries). She bought Laurel a cardigan with porcelain buttons, a green vellum book and fountain pen, *The Golden Compass*, ribbed stockings. Nina is good at presents; she made a career out of having perfect taste. She thinks of Laurel's responsiveness as akin to physical chemistry. Why exactly Nathan's hands make electricity travel along Nina's skin is unfathomable, too—can only be inadequately explained by pointing to stimuli like shirts.

Eleven-year-old Laurel struck Nina as a cat, winding herself around her legs. She reminded Nina of what her mother, always cynical but more so after her divorce, says about cats: "They have a knack for seeking out the one person who doesn't like them." Laurel has her dad's pretty hazel eyes; she asks, deferentially, what book she should read next. Within the parameters of Thanksgiving breaks or weekend trips to the Bay Area, Nina has always enjoyed petting Laurel.

Fourteen-year-old Laurel is another sort of cat altogether. She's practically feral.

☾

"Alice can't cope," Nathan told Nina, when he came back from visiting Berkeley in April, freaked out about his skeletal, miserable daughter. "We need to take Laurel for part of the summer, to see if we can help. See if we can get her back on track."

They were sitting on the couch, drinking wine, watching Jonah roll around his exercise mat. Lying on his back, Jonah reached up to grab one of the toys suspended on the plastic arch above him, a cloth turtle. Nina watched his fingers clutch and miss.

Laurel in her house for a month?

Fairytales are notoriously hard on stepmothers, so Nina had recast herself as a fairy godmother. On Laurel's short visits, she waved her wand to magic up, instead of ballgowns or pumpkin-chariots, a set of German markers with ten different shades of green; she taught Laurel how to bake scones. But a whole month of a depressed teenager with an eating disorder? The thought made Nina's mind go blank, an exposed photograph.

"Alice can't cope," Nathan repeated.

It was a familiar comment, but it wasn't delivered in his familiar tone: derisive, inviting Nina to mock messy, inept Alice. Even before Nathan continued, "We need to give Alice a break," Nina processed that he was speaking not out of scorn, but out of sympathy.

☾

"You can't just leave her with me," Nina says, as Nathan puts on his jacket.

"Nina, I have to work."

"But I am not responsible—."

He's out the door before she can finish the sentence.

In the kitchen after Nathan flees, Nina mashes bananas for Jonah. (He has four teeth now, but still only wants pureed food. He inspects Cheerios and the other finger food Nina scatters on his highchair tray as if they were diamonds, or bird bones. They are interesting to examine from various angles, but he refuses to put them in his mouth.)

Nina considers her sentence, trying to come up with the words that might complete it. "I am not responsible," fill in the blank. For your daughter? Nina catches herself introducing Laurel to people as "Nathan's daughter," rather than "my stepdaughter."

The truth is, Nina could have just ended the sentence, "I am not responsible," period. She is, after all, Nina Durante (now Durante-Haven): Nina who crashed her college suitemate's Mazda (this is partly why ten years later Nina organized Cathy's party, practically for free; she owes that woman a car); who before their college commencement ceremony, as they were lining up in their caps and gowns, did lines of coke with Manuel, her good friend and classmate long before he became her business partner, never mind that it was ten a.m.; who ended up in Portland, Oregon, back in 2008 because she followed a musician boyfriend there. Nina is organized (her scrapbook catalogs every food Jonah has ever sampled, in chronological order), but she has never been responsible.

There's a reason Nathan, four years ago, was so alluring to her, beyond the beacon-like shirt, which has probably gotten via nostalgia too much credit. He was willing to give up everything, wife, kid, firm, for her; to move six hundred miles, for her. For once, Nina was the magnet, rather than the metal filament being drawn; that power exerts its own kind of compulsion (being compelled by one's capacity to compel).

Now Nina, who has never, for fuck's sake, been anyone's notion of responsible, has to look after not just her own thirteen-month-old, but a fourteen-year-old girl who is as skinny as a carrot-peeler, whose mother is a nut, whose father has no idea how to talk to her. Laurel may not in any fair sense be her responsibility, but she is without doubt Nina's problem.

☾

"God, the tension in this house: It's like buttah," says Manuel, when he comes over, doing the Jewish-mom-from-the-Bronx accent that he and Nina have used with each other, for obscure reasons, since they first met as freshmen at Princeton.

Nina sighs. "Can I come back to work? Pretty please?"

"Seriously? Because you know I could use the help. I am very willing to exploit your desire to escape that kid and Mr. America, if you're serious."

Nina contemplates Manuel. He's still beautiful—he is one of those men who will always be beautiful, even when he's old, and has a mane of snowy hair—but at thirty-four, his age is starting to show. Under his eyes are blue shadows. One of the twin daughters of his ridiculous wife doesn't sleep. Nina can't remember if it's Ulrike or Heidi, but one of the two ends up in his bed almost every night, jabbing him with her propeller limbs. This kid is six now, but the wife (Nina doesn't like to think of Elizabeth by name) lets her sleep between them almost every night, and wimpy Manuel won't put his foot down.

Manuel first entered the grownup land of marriage and step-parenting. Nina was perfectly happy being single before Manuel fell in love with absurd, married Elizabeth. At first Nina hadn't taken the affair seriously. Since their days at Princeton, she'd seen Manuel with any number of WASPy girls. Half of them had boyfriends. She was fully prepared once again to offer a shoulder, to pour Manuel wine and laugh about some narrow, *commedia dell'arte* escape through an upstairs window, scaling down lattice work, at the sound of the husband's car in the driveway.

But this time he surprised her: Elizabeth left her husband, and suddenly Manuel was a stepfather of sticky, insomniac twins.

In the sixteen years she's known him, Nina has never so much as kissed Manuel. There was a tacit sense in college that the two Latin kids, so visibly brown at Princeton, should be friends rather than lovers. "Spread the sparkle," said Manuel, their freshman year.

But when people said to them, "You two will end up together someday," and she had laughed and rolled her eyes, Nina nonetheless believed they very well might. She could even picture their *New York Times* Vows profile in the Sunday *Style* section: friends and business partners for years who suddenly looked at each other and realized, You're the one. Until the advent of the wife, she had thought Manuel believed this, too.

Two months after Manuel's desertion through marriage, Nina met Nathan.

"I don't know what to do," says Nina, stretching out her hand, and Manuel, after a pause, pats it.

"Poor girl," he says.

Nina says, "Who are you calling girl, boy?"

Then she sees Manuel is looking out the glass doors, watching Laurel on all fours, crawling with Jonah on the grass.

☾

Laurel is sweet with Jonah, whom she hasn't seen since Thanksgiving, when he was six months old. She gets him to eat non-mashed food, an irony which Nina contemplates: This emaciated girl, who cuts her own food into pieces and then smaller pieces, finally entices Jonah to put a feared Cheerio in his mouth.

"How'd you do it?" asks Nina, amazed.

A trip to the community center and pool is a proposition for which separate imperatives need balancing. On the one hand, it is horrifying to see Laurel in a bathing suit, her ribs on countable display. But once Nina settles on a lawn chair and watches Laurel hold Jonah by the armpits and bob him up and down in the water, she feels less conscious of judgmental eyes. Laurel sweeps Jonah's hair out of his eyes. It's getting too long, but Nina can't bear to cut it.

("Get that kid a haircut," Nathan said one night at dinner, and Nina and Laurel both said "No!" at the same time, then glanced at each other, surprised.)

Laurel is having so much fun that Nina wants to take her place. Even though Nina feels self-conscious in a bathing suit these days—more than a year after pregnancy her stomach is still soft and flabby, webbed with silver stretch marks—Nina gets in the pool. After twenty minutes Jonah is hungry, so they get out. She opens the Tupperware of Cheerios, but Jonah pushes them away. The last Nina looked, Laurel was reading, but now she's gone. Her beach towel is draped on a slatted lawn chair.

Nina lifts Jonah onto her hip. The door to the community center is cracked open, and when Nina looks in, she sees a group of people sitting in folding chairs, watching a speaker at the podium. Or rather, "speaker": it takes Nina a second to realize that the people are deaf, the woman in the front is signing. Bouncing Jonah on her hip to keep him quiet, Nina watches, first the woman and then Laurel, sitting in the back row. After a minute the woman stops signing. The people in the audience raise their hands and flutter their fingers.

Now Laurel catches Nina's eye. "Did you see?" Laurel whispers, when they leave the room. "Did you see how they applaud?"

☾

From another doorway, Nina spies on Laurel and Jonah, playing with his terrible toy. Laurel turns the crank, churning out music. Nina braces herself for the harlequin clown to burst from its metal box. Pop goes the weasel. Even as a child, Nina hated that toy: the way it would bob on its spring, arms outstretched, cheeks rouged, its expression deranged.

☾

One of the goals of this summer is to get Laurel interested in food again, to alchemize food (more wand work) into pleasure instead of a minefield. So Nina asks Laurel to help her bake a *tarte tatin*. She tells Laurel to squeeze lemon on the vellum-thin slices of green apple.

"Why?"

Nina has to look at the girl closely to realize that this is not sulky backtalk. It strikes her that she hasn't heard Laurel ask a real question all June.

But she used to: The pretty girl Nina first met four years ago was full of questions. Mostly about quality: What made that piece of cured meat more expensive than this one? Why were those boots $300? "Feel how soft this leather is," Nina said. "Can you taste how much sweeter and more buttery this prosciutto is than the Spanish one?" Laurel was so invested in learning, and the experience of being an information-delivery system was so gratifying, that it was hard for Nina to spot the landmine questions, the ones she needed to deflect, or to answer only cautiously: "Why did you fall in love with my father?"

Now, Nina explains that the lemon preserves the apples in an acid shield. Otherwise, the apple will turn brown and bruise.

Laurel looks struck. Her eyes widen, as if Nina has told her something very private.

Nina shows Laurel how to layer the apple slices, each C curling into another C, working from the outer circumference to the center. Laurel overlaps them by just two millimeters, the way Nina demonstrated. It takes her a long time to get to the center. When she does, Laurel hesitates, her fingers suspended.

"Is it OK if the last apple slice is horizontal instead of vertical?"

Nina nods. When Laurel places it on, Nina says, "It's a moustache!"

Laurel looks up, and Nina recognizes the look: This time it's Laurel checking her expression for mockery or disdain.

At dinner that night, Nathan compliments the tarte, and Laurel beams. Nina watches her lips close around the tines of her fork.

☾

When Nina first found out she was pregnant with Jonah, after three months of trying, she couldn't reach Nathan all morning. On a construction site, he had turned off his cell. She had other people to call—her mother, her father, Manuel—but none of them could be told until she alerted Nathan that they were having a baby.

This time Nina feels no need to follow such protocols. As soon as she pees on the white stick and sees the double lines, she calls Nathan. Again, he doesn't pick up.

She finds Laurel in the second bedroom, which Nina now thinks of as Laurel's room. Laurel has her back to her. She is brushing her hair, looking at herself in the mirror.

"Hey, Laurel, I have some news."

While she tells her, Laurel watches Nina's eyes in the mirror. "Wow," says Laurel, and then, "Congratulations."

"Thank you! I thought I might be, because everything was starting to smell terrible. Like people had poured buckets of urine on the street."

Laurel hiccup-laughs. "Have you told Dad?"

"Nope, I couldn't reach him. You're the first." Nina takes the brush from Laurel's loose fingers. "Do you mind?" She starts to brush Laurel's hair. "I hope she's a girl. I could name her after you."

"You want to name her Laurel?"

Nina feels a pang. It might be her fault, after all, that Laurel regards herself as so very disposable: that it's within the realm of possibility that her half-sister would have not just her last name, but also her first.

"No, I was thinking about Daphne."

Braiding Laurel's thin, fine hair, Nina tells her the story of Daphne. A nymph, she attracted the attention of the god Apollo. "People think these nymphs and mortals are so honored to have a god infatuated with them, so happy to fall into the god's arms. But half the time, that's not the case. The girls say no, but the gods don't give a crap. They want what they want."

"So what happens?"

"Well, the gods rape them." Nina feels Laurel stiffen. She pauses to get a better grip on Laurel's hair, then continues the story. "So this nymph, Daphne, ran away from pursuing Apollo, and called on her father to help her. Her father was a river god, I forget his name. To stop Daphne from being captured, he changed her into a laurel tree."

Laurel turns her head so suddenly that her hair pulls loose from Nina's fingers. "Seriously? That's the best her father could do? Turn his daughter into a tree? Does she have to stay a tree forever?" When Nina nods, Laurel says, "You're kidding!"

For some reason, Laurel's outrage hits Nina as hysterical. She laughs; she can't stop laughing. After a minute, Laurel laughs, too. It has been years, Nina thinks—since before her marriage, since before Manuel met his beautiful, stupid wife, when they used to go out clubbing together and found themselves in some corner at three in the morning, Nina laughing so hard Manuel had to hold her upright, laughing so hard she felt boneless—it has been years since she has laughed like this. Laurel says, "Why not conjure up a motorcycle? Or a get-away chariot?" and Nina loses control all over again.

The two of them wipe tears from their eyes. "Fathers," Laurel says, shaking her head.

"But listen, there's more," Nina says, and tells her about the laurel tree. Its leaves were used to crown victors. Roman emperors wore wreaths of laurels; so did Olympic athletes. She says, "So your name is a symbol of victory, of achievement."

Laurel looks at Nina. It's the most searching look she's given her all month. Nina holds her gaze, and Laurel must find something in her eyes, some answer to a silent question, because after a minute, Laurel nods.

Nina puts down the brush. Laurel's half-braided hair is unravelling. With both her hands, Nina places an invisible wreath on top of Laurel's head. Nina envisions Laurel surrounded by the roomful of deaf people from the community center. They stand around Laurel in a circle, their arms raised, fluttering their fingers in silent applause.

INSIDE THE BOX

Waiting for you to call me back, contemplating, per usual, the conundrum that is you, it finally dawns. You don't give a shit.

You know how people talk about a light bulb going off? Well, the light bulb here is one of those sad, energy-saver fuckers, where the light is amber and spills, more like beer than light. You can see the tangled filament inside the bulb; its curved walls are smoky.

I make myself say it out loud. You don't give, you don't give, you don't give a shit. It's percussive, a hopeless "Row, Row, Row Your Boat."

I picture myself on a sidewalk. You're walking by in herringbone pants, blue-gray and charcoal. Your shirt is crisply buttoned, and you're holding coffee. You are so put together, I want to spring. I want to spill your coffee; I want to rattle you.

But I can't screech, because I'm the pathetic mime on the corner. In front of me there's a tin cup; inside sits one pleated dollar bill. I wear mime makeup. I'm wondering, for the first time in my thirty-one years, why mimes are monochromatic. What is the relationship between their white face-paint and black lips and their muteness? Why has it never occurred to me that mimes are clowns with the volume violently turned off?

I gesticulate wildly. My gloved hands spiral like the blades of a fan, I'm trying so hard to communicate.

But you walk by, wearing pants so elegant I have to call them "trousers." If you are conscious in the periphery of your vision of the disturbance that is me, mime-palpitating invisible walls, you are so skillful at ignoring me (my climbing palms; my emails; my texts) that the surface of your coffee as you walk by isn't agitated.

And it "comes to me" (a rocket ship, nose-diving in the cratered sphere of my brain). You are so polite, you can't admit to being indifferent to a woman you are fucking. So you must look me in the eyes when you are inside me; you must (eventually) return my calls, and answer my third or fourth email in a row, and say, "Sweetheart."

But the truth is (this truth is the toffee core of a tootsie pop, perfectly visible; let me mouth it at you with my black, stretched mime lips, as you stroll smoothly by), you never, ever gave a shit.

WATCH YOURSELF

There are three relevant facts that Rachel knows about Percy Callahan, now Percy Chazz. One she has known for sixteen years; the other two she more recently added to her imaginary data file on Percy. Really it's more of an imaginary shoebox, and these facts are stored mementos, like sea glass, or the intact shell of an urchin.

One: Percy should have been a twin, but he strangled his twin brother in utero. Or rather, the umbilical cord strangled the twin, but for reasons best known to himself, Percy has always claimed agency for this act. "I killed my twin," he told her, solemnly, when he was seventeen.

Two: In his mid-twenties, Percy married a woman who fancied herself a singer, and who had legally changed her name to Jacaranda Chazz, a character in a 1940s novel. So in love was Percy Callahan with this ridiculous woman, that he changed his own surname to "Chazz." Rachel finds this information baffling. It doesn't square with the seventeen-year-old Percy she remembers, who would change nothing, not even his shirt, for some girl.

Three: Percy and Jacaranda Chazz adopted two African-American boys. This last fact also does not match Rachel's image of the teenage Percy, blond and self-dazzled.

Who is this guy? Rachel has thought over the years, when she ran into some mutual acquaintance from the prep school she and Percy both attended, from which she eventually got kicked out, and they filled her in. Percy sounded wholly unrecognizable.

So it's predictable that when Rachel sees Percy for the first time in fifteen years at an AA meeting in San Francisco, she doesn't recognize him, not even when he introduces himself to the group, "Hello, I'm Percy." She merely intones with the rest of them, "Hello, Percy." It isn't until he says, "I trace my struggles with alcohol to something that happened before I was even born. When I was in utero, I strangled my twin," that Rachel's head snaps up: Percy Chazz! Self-aggrandizing as ever!

After the meeting she approaches and says, "Percy."

He peers at her, and Rachel realizes that she herself may be unrecognizable. The last time he saw her she was fifteen, with braces from which she once had to unthread one of his pubic hairs. But just as she is about to say her name, he says, "Rachel Vicksburg!" and they awkwardly hug.

They go to Samovar, a tea joint around the corner. Percy raises his eyebrows when he sees the prices. "Eight dollars for a pot of tea! Seriously? San Francisco," he says, shaking his head. But he takes out his wallet, because Rachel stands with her arms resolutely crossed.

They sit. The wood of the table seems brighter and yellower than ordinary wood, like it's made from a tree that grew in the Winkie country of Oz.

"So you don't live here?" says Rachel, pouring tea.

"Nope, we live in Austin." Rachel notes how quickly he deploys the pronoun "we." "I'm here for a conference." Percy starts talking about straw-bale houses and solar panels.

The truth is, thirty-three year old Percy is a yawn. If Percy were a guy she saw on Tinder, Rachel would scroll right past him. She would think, "Zzz." His absurd last name should have another "Z" tacked onto it.

He is fascinating only in a historical way, because she adored him when she was a lowly freshman and he was a glamorous senior. He cheated on his high-achieving, Harvard-bound girlfriend with Rachel. Well, "cheated": Rachel never had sex with him. But he was the first boy to suck her nipples. When he visited during her sophomore year, shortly before Rachel got expelled, she gave him her first blowjob. This she did so awkwardly (the dangling pubic hair in her braces needed to be fished out like a parsley stem), that her roommate Caroline Keppler referred to it as a "blow-it job."

He was the first meaningful dot in Rachel's line of boys. Over the years, she has regarded Percy as initiating a pattern: her selection of guys, golden like the weird, unnatural wood of their table, who fuck her and scold her and turn away, eventually, in disgust.

"Do you ever go to reunions?" Percy says.

Rachel shakes her head. "No. I got kicked out a couple of weeks after I last saw you."

"Oh, right, I heard that." He frowns. "Remember, I told you to watch yourself."

He had indeed told her to watch herself. "What's a sophomore doing on probation?" he asked her, when he saw her on the sidelines of a lacrosse game. (Rachel could give a shit about lacrosse, but she'd heard Percy was on campus, visiting from Penn, and she knew where to find the former lacrosse captain.) Translation: What's a bad girl like you doing in a place like this? He told her to watch herself, but that night they drank bourbon from his initialized hip flask. He unzipped his fly, and tangled his fingers in her hair.

"That school was the worst," Rachel says.

Suddenly they're arguing, because the school has been in the news lately. Even if he has changed his last name to "Chazz" and adopted two African-American kids and is doing something-or-other with straw-bale houses, Percy is still enough of a loyal alumnus to scoff when Rachel says, "Rape culture."

"Oh, come on!" Rachel says. "Don't you remember casino night? When they'd set up those roulette wheels and the seniors would gamble with fake money, and you'd all dress up in pseudo-Western, and the freshmen girls would wear Playboy bunny outfits, and we'd serve you popcorn balls on trays? We were supposed to be so honored that we were chosen to be the bunnies!"

The truth is, she had been honored; Caroline, Maggie, Imogen, Bonnie, and Allison, she can still name each of the other girls the senior boys picked. She remembers crowding in front of the dormitory mirror, applying lipstick.

"There's a picture of me in the yearbook, in that bunny outfit," Rachel says. The picture is, in fact, of Percy, in a white Stetson, one arm around Rachel, one arm around Caroline. The caption under it says, "Percy's pets." Memory is a weird thing: Rachel's thirty-year-old self bristles in outrage, even as she remembers Percy's arm around her shoulder, the heat of his skin through her leotard. "I should sue those fuckers," Rachel says.

Percy shakes his head. "You were always a troublemaker."

Rachel remembers Percy looking at her with this same aggrieved expression, fifteen years ago—"Watch yourself"—hours before unzipping his fly.

In fact, it's as if she's obeying his command retroactively, because while she looks at his set, annoyed face, she does watch herself: fourteen-year-old Rachel puckering her lips to apply, inexpertly, Maggie Robinson's red lipstick; fifteen-year-old Rachel stepping out of her jeans, the cold, wet grass of the playing field under her bare ass, while Percy fingered her; and the chaotic course of her life ever since. Percy is the first flame touched to the gasoline trail of alcohol: she pictures gasoline rather than bourbon pouring out of his silver flask, initialized P.B.C., igniting the bonfire of her twenties.

The picture makes her want to see any other image, even confusing ones. So Rachel asks him if he has a family, pretending she doesn't already know (though perhaps her information is out of date; time moves fast for alcoholics).

Percy's irritated expression disappears. He smiles and pulls out his cell phone to show pictures. "Geoffrey is six, Damian is four. They were brothers, getting bounced around in the foster care system. We adopted them three years ago."

"Cute." Rachel can't see well, but there is no way she is putting on her glasses in front of Percy Chazz.

"Do you have kids?" he says.

But Rachel can't bear to tell him about Lia, living with her dad in Los Angeles. Lovely, four-year-old Lia whom Rachel is only allowed to see on supervised visits, whose name Rachel imagines on pale wooden Scrabble squares and rearranges to spell, "Ail." She shakes her head.

Percy says, "And here's my wife. She's a singer." He speaks proudly; it reminds Rachel of the way he told her his girlfriend Dede got into Harvard.

The temptation to bring the blurry face into focus is so strong that Rachel puts on her glasses. Associations are tricky phenomena. Next time she walks past a jacaranda tree—or what Rachel has thought of, for the past two years, since bumping into her old roommate Caroline Keppler

and getting the lowdown on Percy, as a "Jacaranda Chazz"
tree—she will have a face to put to its blue, flowering name.

SUBJECT: LAY OFF THE LAYS

Larry, emailing because you aren't in your office, despite the fact that we have a division meeting in forty-five minutes and you've skipped the last three. Whatever. My question for you is, why must my office hours be spent handing Kleenex to some wailing girl? Am I really the appropriate person to assuage the latest heart you've broken? And their hearts all break in precisely the same way, along the same fault line, as if these girls were mass produced. They might disagree about the metaphysical poets, but they all have the same fidgety feet that swing like metronomes, and the same susceptibility to you. I must say, I feel very little identification. I would never cry in the office of a virtual stranger who has a stack of papers to grade. I would never tell someone with whom prior conversations had been limited to Donne's Holy Sonnets that I wanted to die. Die fucking elsewhere! is what I want to tell these girls. Crawl down the hall to Larry Avanti's office, and expire on his threshold. "I know you and Professor Avanti are friends," they say (funny how they refer to you by title). That's how they always start. "But," they say, and I scramble for Kleenex. Seriously, Larry: I'm tired. "Talk to him," I told this latest iteration, and she said you avoid her. She tried to call, she said, but your wife picked up. Without meaning to, I nodded. I know how quickly Veronica can get to a damn phone, as if she has caster wheels instead of feet. Why don't they have some dignity, poor things? I did, for fuck's sake. No one saw me shed a tear over you. And why don't you exert some restraint? I hardly care anymore; the students are Veronica's problem. Except they bawl in my office, except they have some strange intuition about you and me that surfaces in the conscious thought that I might have influence over you: "I know you and Professor Avanti are friends." So, on the off-chance they are right, I'm asking you, as a "friend," to stop fucking the undergrads, at least the ones in my classes, to stop cracking them down the middle, because for God's sake, Larry, I can't suture them, or protect you.

PERNE IN A GYRE

Nan has not spoken to her father for nearly nine months. Their most recent telephone conversation at Christmas lasted less than ten minutes. (He asked her if she had received her present, a pair of cashmere socks Nan knew his wife Greta must have picked out. Every time Nan opens her bureau drawer, she feels freshly irritated that her father got her socks for Christmas.)

So Nan knows something is up as soon as she hears her father's voice, flat and atonal. She knows before he says, "Listen, Cakes, I have bad news." Her mother is sick, he tells her. She fainted in her tai chi class.

"They have tai chi in Oklahoma?" Nan says, stalling. Her mother told her about the class weeks ago. Nan teased her, making up names for poses: the Ferocious Crane, the Eager Watermelon.

He ignores the question. When her mother came to, he tells Nan, she was lying on the floor with her feet elevated. A woman in the class was holding her wrist, taking her pulse. Maureen did not want to go to the hospital, but the paramedics insisted. At first, it seemed like no big deal. Fainting happens to older people, the attending nurse said. "You're probably just dehydrated." Maureen drank water and chatted with the nice male nurse about the novel he was reading. But after the blood test results, everyone became somber. Maureen's white blood cell count was high. So there were more tests, and a sonogram, and, finally, the diagnosis.

"It started in her colon, but it has metastasized into her bones. And for some damn reason, I'm her emergency contact. God knows why. We've been divorced ten years. That contact should be you." Her father bites off the words, though Nan isn't sure at whom the accusation is levelled: her mother, for never bothering to change her information, or Nan, for being 6,000 miles away.

Nan pictures her brain as a clear cage of stuffed toys in an arcade; she pictures a drop claw, stretching and descending to select a question. "Is Mom OK?"

"Of course she isn't OK, Nan! She has stage four cancer. She's dying." Her father sighs. "Listen, Cakes: you need to come home."

Holding the phone to her cheek, Nan considers *home*. The word seems as alien as *metastasized*. "Home" certainly doesn't describe Muskogee, Oklahoma, where her father, now in Denver, no longer lives himself; where Nan grew up, where she fled sixteen years ago for college. Now she barely visits. Nan last saw her mother a year ago when Maureen came to Tokyo. The only Japanese thing her mother liked to eat was pickled ginger, which she ate by the forkful, and the packages of dried seaweed with which Nan stocks her cabinets. Haru doesn't like her apartment to smell like cooking

Nor does "home" describe Tokyo, though Nan has lived in this studio apartment for nearly three years.

In fact, Nan has spent the last five days, prior to this phone call, trying to develop an exit plan, while lying on her king-sized bed that disproportionately fills the room. (There's also a bureau and a wicker rocking chair, a bathroom with glass tiles the color of celery, and the tiny kitchen Nan hardly ever uses.)

"This place looks like a hotel room," her mother said when she saw her apartment, puzzled. "Not a place where someone lives."

When her father hangs up, Nan feels, under the concrete slab of misery, a weed-shoot of relief. Now she has a reason to leave that Haru will not object to, conscientious Japanese son that he is. Of course Nan has never met Haru's parents, but she knows he visits them every Sunday. Haru refuses to talk about his wife. He speaks of Matsumi only in pronouns, as when he mentioned a film that "someone" he knew had seen. When Nan, antennae alert, asked if it was good, Haru said, carefully, "They liked it." To find out anything at all about Matsumi, Nan must resort to subterfuge. But Haru freely shares information about his parents. Nan knows Haru brings his mother a box of sesame candy every Sunday. When Haru described these candies, his elegant fingers shaped cylinders out of air.

Nan calls Haru at work, something she is supposed to do only in case of emergency. For a long time she is on hold. His voice is terse when he gets on the phone. "What is it?"

As soon as Nan says "My mother has cancer," tears flood; her nose runs. She is taken aback by how many fluids she exudes.

Haru's voice becomes soft and buttery. "Of course, of course. Take as long as you need." He gives her his travel agent's number. "Atsuko has my credit card information. Leave your return open. Tell her you want to go business class."

"Thank you," Nan says. When she travels with Haru, they fly first class. She has gone on three trips with Haru, to Rome, to New Zealand, to Bali, but the only memories the drop-claw in her brain can snatch from those trips is the voyage there: the white cloth napkins, the glass flutes of champagne.

☾

"Take my room," her mother tells her, but Nan refuses. There is no way she could fall asleep in the queen bed that belonged to her parents, facing the bureau that still, inexplicably, has a framed picture of the three of them, Nan, her mother, her father, at Nan's high school graduation. The picture certainly wasn't there five years ago, the last time Nan visited. Her mother must have tucked it into some drawer before picking up Nan at the airport. Now, stuck in the hospital, Maureen has not been able to spend days baking blondies and seven-layer-bars, sticky with condensed milk. She has had no opportunity to hide anything incriminating, anything that will stoke Nan's concern or pity.

What is most depressing? The fact that her mother still displays this pretend-family shot? Or that she conceals it from Nan? Or that Nan's face in the picture is unlined, her eyes as wide as a fawn in a Disney movie?

Instead, Nan sleeps in her old room, crowded with her mother's sewing machine and dozens of bolts of fabric: fabric that will never be made into the skirts and blouses and summer dresses her mother planned.

These unmade clothes float like ghosts.

Nan has to pick her way through a forest of fabric bolts, lemonade yellow, red and white checked, or the most disturbing of all: a mint-green background with bunches of balloons. That one must have been chosen for non-existent grandchildren. Once, when she still lived in San Francisco, Nan took her mother to a fabric shop in the Sunset district.

According to Yelp reviews, it was famous for retro prints. Her mother ran her finger over fabric obviously intended for children: sturdy cottons depicting gingerbread men, rocket ships, robots. When Maureen saw Nan watching her, she blushed.

☾

"How long will you be there?" Haru emails her.

Nan can only get an Internet connection in the basement of the house. She sits cross-legged on the shag carpet, her laptop propped on the coffee table where, in high school, she and her friends Gabrielle, Sunny, Roy, and Patrick used to set Patrick's skull-head bong. Nan remembers crawling on the rug, looking for marijuana buds that someone had spilled.

"The doctors say three months, maybe less."

Nan can type these words without crying, though if speaking them, she would be the same water-logged mess she was in Tokyo. She told her father this timeline the same way, in an email including links to the Mayo Clinic. Her father wrote back, "Sorry, Cakes." She imagined him dry-eyed, reading his email while Greta poached chicken for dinner.

"Let me know if there is anything I can do," Haru emails.

Nan is tempted to make outrageous requests: "Come to Oklahoma! Meet my mother! Keep me sane while my mother dies!"

While her mother shrinks away might be more accurate. Maureen is becoming visibly smaller, harder. She's like a strip of meat hung to cure. When Nan holds her hand, it feels less warm and pliable than flesh. Her mother's body is already in process of transforming into something other than a body: a piece of petrified wood, a polished tusk.

☾

Time stretches like the dachshund toy Nan had as a kid: Its head and front legs were joined to its hindquarters and tail by a Slinky. As a child, Nan believed that the toy was in pain every time his front half was separated from his back half. She could only play with it when tightly compressing the two halves.

Nan scrolls through Facebook, searching for anyone still in Muskogee. Not Sunny, who lives in Kentucky now and has seven-year-old twins. She constantly posts pictures of their jack-o-lantern faces. Not Patrick, finishing his radiology residency in Los Angeles. Nan remembers making out with Patrick in this basement. They never really dated: He was too goofy. But it's clear from his profile picture that he has aged well. He used to wind Nan's watch for her, a watch with a red alligator strap. Gabrielle is not on Facebook. Roy is still in town, though, and after Nan sends him a message, he invites her over for dinner.

He hugs Nan when she rings the doorbell. "Look at you! You look exactly the same."

Roy looks as if he's been inflated. Nan says, "You," meaning to say "You, too," but her awareness of this—that even Roy's head seems fatter—makes her sentence grind awkwardly to a halt. "You have such a nice house," Nan finishes, stupidly.

Roy nods. "Denise, come say hello."

"So pleased to meet you," says Nan to a freckled woman with rabbity teeth.

Roy and Denise shake their heads. "We've met," says Denise.

It turns out they were in high school together, though it's five minutes later, after Denise has enumerated context after context (Mr. Dashwood's history class; yearbook; some school play), that Nan's memory finally clicks: She pictures Denise with silver face-paint, a fairy to Nan's queen, offering in cupped hands an imaginary honeycomb.

"You were in *A Midsummer Night's Dream*."

"Right, I was Peaseblossom," says Denise. "And you were Titania. Do you still act?"

"A little."

"And model, too, right?" says Denise.

"That's right." Denise is a sunlamp warming Nan. Under the beam of Denise's questions, Nan feels glamorous and interesting: San Francisco, Japan, mostly film these days, not stage.

Of course, when Denise asks, "You mean movies?" Nan has to admit, no, commercials.

In one ad, she was a girl in a bar, "Which is funny, because I don't even drink."

"*You* don't drink?" Roy says, raising his eyebrows.

"Not really." Nan remembers, suddenly, being wasted, and Roy holding her hair back while she vomited on the grass. Was it his lawn? Patrick's?

"And I was a sorority girl, in another one," Nan continues, to dissolve this image of Roy gripping her hair.

"You should see if they're casting at the community theater," Denise says.

Dinner is chicken and rice filled with weird, sweet things, raisins and lentils, which Nan locates, avoids eating, and then buries under more rice. Roy pours her wine and then says, "Oh, sorry, I forgot." He adds her wine to his own glass.

The gratification produced by Denise's attention evaporates as they talk. Patrick is chief resident of his hospital in L.A., Roy tells her; his pretty, blond wife is an obstetrician. Nan tells him she went to grad school. For what? An MFA in poetry. Once more, Roy looks baffled.

Denise says, "Oh yes, I remember your poems! You had poems in *The Starlight*!" (Nan would never have been able to reproduce, never mind so swiftly, the name of their high school literary magazine). "Are you published?"

And the glow once again disperses as Nan says, "No." This unspools into a long string of nos. No, Nan doesn't have kids. No, she is not married. No, she doesn't have a boyfriend.

Nan is so habituated to Haru being a secret that this last "no" pops out before she can stop herself. Afterwards she longs to retract it, just like the disclosure about not drinking. She watches Roy refill his glass. She wants to sip wine and tell them stories about Haru, her handsome, cultured boyfriend, who takes her on trips all over the world.

☾

"I saw Roy last night. Remember Roy Petersen?"

"Of course!" her mother says. "I have cancer, not Alzheimer's."

Her mother picks an ice chip from her cup, puts it on her tongue, and grimaces. For some reason—Nan doesn't know if it's the disease or the medication—everything tastes bitter to her mother, even water. Ice is better ("The cold is distracting, anyway"), but not much.

"So how is Roy? Still fat?"

This makes Nan laugh, then stop. These sharp edges are not like her mother. Maureen was the sweet, courteous yin to her father's brusque yang, though she never scolded her husband for being rude or critical, other than sighing, "Oh, John." It was Nan whom she tried to polish and soften, Nan whom she told, "Be polite," "There's no harm in kindness," "If you can't say something nice, don't say anything at all."

Has cancer made her mother bitter, like the ice chips? Or is this harshness the product of something else?

When Nan smoothed the covers on her mother's bed, she noticed a depression in the middle of the bed, indicating where her mother has been sleeping: no longer on the far left, making room for her space-consuming husband. In her own bed in Tokyo, Nan always sleeps on the left, even though Haru hardly ever sleeps over (only when his wife is on vacation with their two children). Perhaps having Nan's father gone—not just divorced, but in Colorado—has made her mother migrate toward the middle in other ways? To cease being the base to neutralize her husband's acid?

"Roy's wife seems nice," Nan says.

"Denise. Yes, she's pleasant." Her mother puts another ice chip in her mouth. "Though a bit silly, don't you think? A bit eager?"

"Oh, Mom," says Nan. She remembers her mother shaking her head, murmuring "Oh, John."

"Her mother's in my book club. Florence Habersham. She always wants to read the most saccharine books! I couldn't even get through the last one." She frowns. "Poor Florence. She's desperate for grandchildren. I don't know why they don't have kids. I don't know if there's a problem there, or …." Her voice trails off.

Nan waits. After a long time, she says, "Or?" But her

mother doesn't respond, and when Nan looks down, Maureen has fallen asleep.

☾

Several days after going to Roy's for dinner, Nan looks up Muskogee Players, the community theater website. They are auditioning for a play: Harold Pinter's *Betrayal*. When she sees the title of the play, Nan bites her lip. It feels like a sign. This is a play she read for Twentieth Century British Literature, one of the two lit classes she took at San Francisco State University for her MFA. Paul's class.

There are only three characters in the play: Robert, his wife Emma, and his best friend Jerry. Emma and Jerry have an affair that lasts seven years. The most distinctive thing about *Betrayal* is that it goes backwards in time. It begins two years after the affair is over, and concludes right before the affair begins. It ends when Jerry grasps Emma's arm and the two characters, unaware of everything to come, of the pain the audience has seen unfold, exchange a look.

Of that ending, Paul said, "Before experience is innocence. Experience is the product time manufactures." Nan remembers writing those words in her mottled notebook.

She feels silly when she gets to the audition, in her red wrap dress and boots. Her black-and-white headshot is four years old, and when Nan gives it to the director, he frowns. She imagines that he is registering how out-of-date the photo is. But Nan likes this picture: no wrinkles around her eyes, her bangs perfectly groomed. When she was living in San Francisco, still modeling, Nan got her bangs trimmed once a week. She kept them on the verge of too long, nearly in her eyes, because a photographer once told her that's how he liked her: hidden. Cate, her one real friend in her MFA program, the one who wasn't dismissive about Nan's writing, who didn't refer to her poems as "efforts," found it hilarious whenever Nan told her she had just gotten a trim. "How much this time? One millimeter?" Cate would ask.

Another woman hands the director a Christmas card for her picture. She says, "Sorry, this is all I have."

☾

Afterwards, Nan is sure she was given the part of Emma because she is pretty, and not because she was impressive. During the audition, Nan had hiccups, and when she held the script, she kept imagining her mother's papery skin.

Mickey, the actor who plays Jerry, her character's lover, is potbellied and flirtatious, despite being married. But Timothy, the actor who plays Robert, her character's husband, is beautiful, in a familiarly asexual way. He reminds Nan of male models. Even when these models were straight, they struck Nan as neutered, with their waxed chests, perfectly groomed eyebrows, and flat, hard abdomens. For Nan, such men were for looking, not touching. Their bodies seemed laminated. They were props to bend oneself around.

So Nan is surprised at how much she looks forward to kissing quiet, beautiful Timothy, the man who plays her husband.

They rarely touch—their marriage in the play is troubled, given that Emma spends most of the play involved with her husband's best friend—so Nan anticipates Scene Four, which ends with Robert/Timothy kissing her. First her character responds; then she breaks away to cry on his shoulder. In the minutes leading up to their kiss, Nan feels her skin warm and thrum. It is hard to follow the stage direction to break away. Nan wants to keep kissing him. Last rehearsal, her reaction was so delayed that Timothy opened his eyes and stared at her.

It has been nearly two months since she last had sex, two months since she saw Haru. Nan needs to remedy this situation before she grabs the sides of Timothy's face with both hands, or before she lets Mickey, who uses his tongue when he kisses her, screw her. She isn't attracted to Mickey. Nan has issues with soft bellies. Besides, he is married.

These days, Nan's physical contact, outside of the scenes with the two men who play her husband and her lover, is limited to her mother: swabbing her mother's forehead with a washcloth, putting ice chips on Maureen's pale tongue.

Nan pictures herself growing soft, brown, rotten.

Since Nan was twelve, since boys first started noticing her, she has needed to be touched, or at least to be viewed, to convince herself that she is here. Otherwise, Nan starts to disappear. In bright sunlight, she imagines one could see through her. Soon she will be a hologram.

Lying in her twin bed at night, surrounded by the bright bolts of fabric that will never get made into clothes, Nan thinks about Haru's hands, dry and cool. Somehow, Haru extracted all moisture and stickiness from sex. Nan always knew when Haru was stopping by: on Mondays and Thursdays. If Haru was making an exceptional visit, he would text her. This was to give Nan a couple of hours to get waxed, to put on the lingerie that filled her bureau drawers. Haru presented lingerie to Nan, always the colors of a fruit cocktail: cantaloupe, pear. He liked to unlock the door and find Nan kneeling on the bed, hand on hip, a pinup. Haru took a long time undressing her, turning her this way and that while he unsnapped, unbuttoned, and unhooked.

The undressing lasted longer than the sex. Afterwards, Nan showered. Only when she was clean and dry, her hair combed, her skin dusted with baby powder (Nan felt like a sugared doughnut), would he kiss her shoulder and say, "My lovely Nan."

In the minutes when Nan waited to hear his key in the door, when she arranged herself on the bed, wiggling her foot to keep it from going to sleep, Nan would think that her relationship with Haru Tatsuo was not all that different from modeling. It involved posing, upkeep. Nan got Brazilian waxes every three weeks, kept herself moisturized and manicured, wore floppy hats to keep her face out of the sun. Haru is mildly repelled by bodies, the fluids they exude, their texture, the way they smell. He likes Nan artificial and composed, a vase of arranged flowers.

☾

"So tell me about him."

Nan looks up from her phone, startled. Maureen's shifts from sleeping to waking have become so stealthy.

"Tell you about who?" Nan says.

Maureen waves her hand, impatiently. "The man in Japan."

"How—?"

"I have cancer, I'm not an idiot."

Nan looks at the opposite wall, painted a watery color she thinks of as "hospital blue." She pictures the way Haru's hair falls into his eyes. Though he is forty-four, his hair is still completely black. Once, when they were lying in bed, he looked at her in a piercing way, as if he were about to say something important, and then plucked a hair from her head. "Gray hair," he said, showing it to her.

"He's married, isn't he?" her mother says. When Nan nods, her mother sighs. "Kids?"

"Two." Nan pauses, then says, "A third on the way."

Haru hasn't told her this. But Nan found the sonogram image in his wallet while he was in the shower. She remembers drawing in her breath so loudly she could picture the speech bubble emerging from her mouth: Gasp! So much for his endless deflections when Nan talks about turning thirty-four, wanting a baby someday.

"I was involved with a married man once." When Nan looks at her, startled, her mother laughs. "You should see your face! You look like a girl in a comic book, gasping!"

Hearing her mother articulate the cartoon image she had just pictured makes Nan close her eyes. States that used to be distinct are fusing: sleeping and waking, living and dying, her body, perched in the scratchy hospital chair, her mother's in the bed.

"It was after Dad and I split up," her mother says. "I went through a nutty time. I remember being in one of those expensive bath stores, and stealing a soap. Speckled, like a robin's egg. I put it in my pocket and walked out. I didn't seem to have an appropriate sense of what did and did not belong to me." She contemplates her bony fingers. "Do you have a picture of this fellow?"

"'Fellow'! You sound like you're in a Victorian novel," Nan says. "No, but I have this." She takes the slip of paper out of her wallet, tucked behind her credit card, and hands it to her mother. Her mother unfolds it, looks at the sonogram, and breaks into a sudden, elated smile.

"Oh, Nan!"

"Mom, it's not mine. It's his. I mean, his wife's. I took it, like you with the soap. I found out she was pregnant, just a few days before I came home."

Home: the word seems to drop and sink inside her, a marble in a chute.

Nan watches her mother's smile disappear. Three months ago, Nan stopped taking her birth control pills. She looked at the pill pinched between her fingers, and instead of putting it in her mouth, she rolled it up in Kleenex and threw it away. She pictures the Kleenex, celery colored to match the titles; she pictures the bone-colored waste basket. She cried when her period started the next month. That was two weeks before she found the sonogram image in Haru's wallet.

Her mother's fingers move. At first Nan thinks she is crumpling the sonogram, but then she sees she's folding it instead, then refolding it, precise, quick pleats. In a minute she hands it back to Nan: an origami boat.

☾

"So your name is Nan, like the bread?"

If a man said this to her in San Francisco, Nan would have felt disdainful. But in Muskogee, the fact that a man knows Indian food charms her.

"Well, you pronounce it Nan," she says.

Ted is cute: surprisingly, cuter than his picture on the website, where half his face was in shadow. Nan used to online date all the time—it was how she met most of her boyfriends, before Haru—but after three years, she's rusty.

She likes Ted's curly hair. It reminds her of Paul's, her professor from years ago. Ted tells her that he wants to travel to Asia, so she takes out her passport and shows him her stamps for Japan and Bali. She tells him about the bar in Bali with the palm-frond roof that served drinks made with loquats, grated ginger, and gin.

"That sounds amazing."

She tells him about the play she's doing and the way it moves backward in time.

"So the audience knows from the beginning that your character and her lover are going to cause each other all this suffering?" he says.

"The audience knows, but the characters don't. So the audience watches them fall in love, and have no sense of what harm is coming. The scenes towards the end are so hopeful." Nan takes a sip of her wine. "Before experience is innocence. Experience is the product time manufactures."

"That's lovely," he says.

Nan opens her mouth to tell him that was Paul's line, her grad school professor. But she stops herself, just as twenty minutes ago she stopped herself from correcting Ted when he referred to them both being thirty. She was about to: It was an innocent mistake. She had said something about graduating in 2004, and it was only after he said, "Oh, me too!" that she realized he meant high school, not college. Then, as now, she opened her mouth, then closed it.

Because she likes being smart, and saying elegant things; she likes being thirty, the past four years erased, Japan evaporated. Her mother fingering those bolts of fabric at the store in the Sunset neighborhood, planning clothes for grandchildren.

Besides: What the hell does that phrase mean, anyway? Paul had a way of drawing out vowels that made his declarations in class sound aphoristic, but later, when Nan thought about them, they didn't make much sense. Paul sounded good; Nan, queen of looking good, recognizes a similar contrivance about him, a self-construction.

"How long are you in town?" Ted asks, and he smiles when she says, Indefinitely.

In the bathroom Nan smiles, too, at her image in the mirror. She reapplies lipstick: Fetish, her favorite shade. Muskogee has things now: cosmetics stores, tai chi classes, theater. It would be possible to make a life here. She wonders if Ted has a garden. As she combs her hair, she thinks of a website that a friend once showed her where you upload your face with your boyfriend's and the images blend to forecast the children you might have. Ted has brown eyes, like hers, though his are not almond shaped. She imagines the pixels of their faces fusing.

When she gets back to the table, though, he is frowning. Her passport is in his hands.

"Why did you lie about your age?" he says.

"Why are you looking at my passport?"

"You left it on the table." He shrugs, as if this answer is adequate. "This seems an inauspicious start, though, to begin by lying. I think I'd better go."

"Wait," Nan says. She wants to explain the misunderstanding about the graduation date, but though Ted looks at her, patiently, no other words emerge. She has a panicky thought: Is she capable of coming up with lines that are not scripted?

Ted stands up, and says quietly, "I'll pay for the drinks."

☾

Nan wakes up the next morning with that feeling of dread that she remembers from her serious drinking days: her mind scrabbling to recall what precisely occurred. Why does she keep thinking of her brain as clawed? But no longer a mechanical drop-claw. Now it is something small and feral: a hamster, scratching at the shredded paper lining its cage.

When the image of Ted walking away returns, she closes her eyes. The whole incident with the passport feels less mortifying than the memory of studying her reflection in the bathroom mirror, thinking about that website that merged couples' faces into blurry, hypothetical children.

Mortified: Nan turns the word over in her hamster-claw mind, considering its root. What is the link between embarrassment and death? Being so embarrassed one wants to die? Or is there something fundamentally embarrassing about death, losing control over one's body? She thinks of a William Butler Yeats poem Paul used to quote, something about the soul being harnessed to a dying animal. Is that why Haru finds bodies so objectionable, why she has to be dry and powdered, perfumed and presented, as if on a tea tray (the tray her bed, with its satin cover)? Because bodies are mortal, so one has to obscure their scent of decay?

Nan has an actor's memory, trained to learn lines quickly but not to retain them. So it is not until her rehearsal that night that the line from the Yeats poem returns to her in full: "Consume my heart away; sick with desire / And fastened to a dying animal."

They are rehearsing Scene Six, the scene where Emma is reunited with Jerry after she has been travelling with her husband for several weeks. Her husband has learned about the affair, but Emma chooses not to tell Jerry that Robert knows. She does not tell Jerry for years, until after her marriage is over. Is her silence an effort to protect him, or is it less defensible? Emma's motives have always seemed obscure to Nan, though now, in her hamster-claw state, they feel intelligible. Emma is fighting to survive, and such actions are inherently selfish.

Scene Six ends with Jerry and Emma lying down in bed, embracing. Mickey sticks his tongue in Nan's mouth, as he has been doing for weeks, and this time Nan returns the kiss. The Yeats line unfurls in her brain like a scroll: *sick with desire*. Her left hand rests on Mickey's ass, which, unlike his belly pressed against hers, feels solid, not fat.

"Throw some water on those two," says Allen, the director.

Later, after Nan has put on her coat, someone comes up behind her and puts his hands on her shoulders. Of course it is Mickey, though he says nothing. He pushes her hair over her left shoulder, and she feels his lips, wet and warm, on the back of her neck. He unbuttons the coat she has just buttoned. Nan raises her arms slightly to give him room. Still kissing the back of her neck, Mickey pulls her shirt out of the waistband of her skirt. His fingers slide up her ribs. He pinches her nipples. She gasps; the heating in the theater is wonky, and Mickey's hands are cold, as cold as her mother's, which, due to Maureen's cancer-wracked circulation, feel carved from stone. His right hand slides down the waistband of her skirt. Nan allows herself a beat of regret that the hand touching her does not belong to beautiful, silent Timothy, the actor who plays her husband.

An hour later, Nan waits at home. Getting ready for Mickey, Nan longs, in the abstract way she wished for his hand to be Timothy's instead, for any of the silky camisoles and teddies that fill her bureau drawers in Japan. She must make do with her black bra and panties. She hasn't brought any robes, so she wears her mother's terrycloth one.

More unsettling still: She is stuck with her mother's bedroom, because her own twin bed is too small.

She looks, impatiently, at the digital clock. Mickey's wife is out of town, visiting her sister, but before he can come over, Mickey has to walk their dog. Wouldn't a more ardent lover forego the dog walk? Risk the possibility of urine to mop up when he arrives home, late and sated? It's an errant thought, dangerous to even consider when she should be psyching herself up to get laid.

To regain her bearings, Nan looks at herself in the mirror over her mother's bed. Her lips are pale: She needs to repaint them.

Suddenly she remembers being in a bar with Paul, four years ago, when she was finally able, after repeated invitations, to lure him out for a drink. "I want to talk to you about my Pinter paper," she said. Paul raised a skeptical eyebrow, but capitulated. She remembers sitting in the bar in the Richmond next to the Korean barbecue, presenting him with a drink: "I'm buying, because you're advising." She remembers Paul twisting his wedding ring, then laughing at something she said. He didn't kiss her, though she had exerted all her mind-control powers to incite him to.

But Paul stretched his hand across the table; he touched her bottom lip. He said, "You're clever." And this moment seems like the end of *Betrayal*, the hopeful point of no return: innocence before experience. That moment of being special, of being regarded. That moment before Paul's eyes turned from Nan's mouth to his fingertip; before he looked surprised to see it lipstick-stained.

SQUIRREL BEACH

Katrine used to be fun, but ever since she got sober she's as boring as the rest of them. Now it's "My sponsor this, my sponsor that." Now family get-togethers are that much more of a fork in my eye.

Before she became the queen of AA, Katrine and I used to hang out on Squirrel Beach, watching the kids splash around the lake. We drank the fancy $7 microbrews that Seth, Katrine's husband and my obnoxious brother, bought at Whole Foods, and we made fun of all the ways my parents' house sucked. Starting with: weren't beaches supposed to be sandy, actually pleasurable to lie on? Not all rocks, so that even when we brought Mom's soft, fluffy towels, the ones that were *absolutely not* for the beach, so we had to sneak them down, it was like lying on piles of acorns? Or the skulls of vertebrates. That was Katrine's theory, that it was called Squirrel Beach because it was some ceremonial, small beast burial ground. She used to make me laugh, Katrine.

Even when we were talking about serious shit. Like the fact that she had fallen for the new teacher at her school. Katrine taught math and science; Victor taught humanities. I forecasted the whole thing. We sat on the beach, watching Katrine's Ronny push around my Claire, haul Claire by the elbow and try to get her to swim to the buoy, and Katrine went on and on about the new teacher. The fact that she was telling me such boring shit was what made me pay attention. Victor brought his own coffee because he didn't like the coffee they stocked in the faculty lounge. She thought that was interesting. Or worth telling, for some reason: that it signified something exceptional about him, some way he rose above the crowd.

Honestly, I thought he sounded pretentious, and kind of like Seth with his precious microbrews. I wondered what it said about Katrine, that she fell for such particular guys. Maybe it made her feel good about herself, that someone choosy would pick her.

Anyway, I saw the whole thing coming, from coffee snob onset. Katrine and I lay on our stomachs, Katrine wearing her giant, Scarlett O'Hara hat, and talked. I felt a little bad for Seth, but I looked forward to those Saturdays, too, to finding out what happened next. When Katrine told me about Victor giving her a blue coffee mug with a gold *fleur-de-lis*, I said, "You know he wants to sleep with you." She shook her head and laughed. They were just friends, she said, and besides, he was married.

I could have said, "So are you," but I didn't.

Because Katrine reminded me of my friend Claire Pederowsky from when I was sixteen. We spent that summer lying on a beach talking about boys, the summer Claire, the prettiest girl in my class, lost her virginity to this boy Scott. I heard every contour of that romance, too: the way he kissed the hollow of her neck; the way the tip of his penis reminded Claire of the silky cap of a mushroom. We were close that summer, though not once school started again. But that summer I watched Claire braid and re-braid her hair, and I listened to her talk.

You expect twenty-nine to feel different from sixteen, but it doesn't, really. I was intrigued and envious just like back then (because you try being a single mother and having any kind of sex life). Every weekend I heard another chapter: from Victor making her coffee, to buying Katrine her own blue mug, to drinks after work, to first kiss, to the hotel room where Victor made her come twice. Katrine alternated between giddiness and suffering, just like Claire.

Well, Katrine's suffering was worse. She fell hard for Victor, and it was clear to me there was no future there. She asked. "Should I leave Seth?" I looked at her beautiful, bloodshot eyes, and I thought about what a dick Seth had been when we were kids.

When Seth found out, Katrine lost it. I heard this part from Seth, not Katrine: how she wrung her hands like someone praying, how she kept saying, "What can I do, what can I do?"

And according to Seth, what followed was like a job negotiation: the kind you have when you're ready to quit, so you ask for the moon to see what they will give you.

"Quit drinking," he told her.

But then Seth looked off to the distance—we were sitting on Squirrel Beach again, me and Seth. My ass was hurting, because we were on some ratty towel that might as well have been a dishcloth. Seth wouldn't sneak out Mom's fluffy towels; he followed her rules. After a pause, Seth staring at the steel-colored lake, he explained that this never would have happened without Katrine drinking. She never would have kissed Victor if she hadn't kicked back two Jack Daniel's. He didn't mention me at all—he never asked me if I knew, or why I didn't tell him. But he looked down at my hand, at the can I was holding. I knew he was picturing me and

Katrine on the beach, lying on our stomachs, whispering. Our heads together, her wearing that wide-brimmed hat.

So, that was a year ago. Katrine got her sobriety chip last week. I saw her show it to my sister Melissa. Melissa said, "Good for you."

Now I'm the only one on Squirrel Beach drinking, and it's cans of Miller Lite. Seth doesn't bring fancy beer, because he's supporting Katrine. Everyone is supporting Katrine.

And Katrine keeps her distance from me. I don't know if it's because of the can in my hand, or because I heard every chapter of her story and never told her to stop. Sometimes it's just me on Squirrel Beach, watching Claire paddle around with Ronny. I see how long-legged Claire is getting. She's eight now; I watch her swim farther and farther out. All I ever wanted was someone who would always love me.

Yesterday Melissa sat next to me, watching the kids. Her two are at sleep-away camp. I said to her what I'd been thinking: "Missy, no one warns you how hard it is to be a single parent."

She said, "I tried, Liz. I tried to warn you."

But she didn't tell me to call her "Melissa," which is what she has said since she went to college and reinvented herself.

Then she tapped my beer can and said, "Maybe you should let up on that." But she said it gently, not in her bitchy, superior way. We watched the kids swim towards the buoy, their arms white scissor blades shearing the water.

THIS MUCH

It was early when Ben woke up. He could tell this from the diluted quality of the bars of light coming through the shutters. Lying in bed, he could hear bustle downstairs, and wafting up (perhaps this was what woke him) was the smell of bacon. It took him a moment to orient himself. He was groggy and thick-headed from the sleeping pill he'd taken last night—damn these Ambien hangovers. He was wearing boxers and a T-shirt because Miriam had shared his bed last night (which also accounted for the sleeping pill). The commotion downstairs at, the bedroom clock confirmed, not quite 7 a.m., when reasonable people should be sleeping in, was attributable to—damn again. Remembering, Ben hoisted himself out of bed and, haste making him clumsy, put on and tied his bathrobe.

Their kitchen was small (its size had been Miriam's biggest concern when they bought the house, twenty-two years ago). Five people made it crowded. At the table were Ben's soon-to-be son-in-law William Applebaum, and Laura Crenshaw, who had been Edith's friend since the two girls were just starting grade school. He remembered those sleepovers, Laura's curious, old-fashioned nightgowns with their flowing sleeves. Miriam and Edith were manning the stove, Edith stirring home fries, Miriam, standing back a little from the pan, cooking bacon. She had tongs in one hand to lift the pieces onto a plate spread with paper towels. Ben watched her, smiling. She held a strip of bacon at arm's length, as if it were a water moccasin.

"Let me do that," he said, after a moment.

Miriam looked at him, grinned. "With pleasure! God. I can't stand the sound of the fat, sizzling." She put the bacon on the plate and handed him the tongs with a kind of flourish.

"Dad!" Edith, his dancing daughter, gave him a bump with her hip as he squashed beside her at the range. "Did we wake you? We were all trying to be very quiet."

"Quiet as a herd of wildebeests," Ben said. "No, you were fine. I would have gone back to sleep, if I hadn't remembered what day it is."

"Shh, don't mention it," Edith said. "We haven't had enough coffee yet to cope. We're all just trying to put it out of mind. This," she announced loudly, pitching her voice like a carny, "is a perfectly ordinary Saturday."

Eye-rolls to this all around, William at the table muttering "Yeah, right," Laura twirling her index finger to indicate lunacy, and only Miriam following the unspooling of a different mental thread. She said aloud, to no one in particular, "If I had a castle, and it was being invaded by, you know, hordes, what I would pour from my ramparts would be bacon fat. Wouldn't that be better than boiling oil? What's scarier than bacon fat?"

"You planning to scald our wedding guests, Mom?" asked Edith.

"Ha! You said the word!" crowed Laura, and Edith raised her hands. She might have been warding off, she might have been gathering.

☾

After breakfast, Ben went outside to look at the tent. "Like a circus," Miriam had said, when it went up two days ago. Inside the tent it was cool. He picked up one of the folding chairs stacked against the wooden floor the carpenters had built. First the ceremony would be here; later, the altar would be cleared for dancing. He unfolded the chair and sat down. He concentrated on the sounds of his breathing. Even breaths. "It's all right," he said aloud. Because the word "right" pleased and soothed him, he repeated it. "We're doing all right."

Normal of course to feel sad at the wedding of a daughter. He was making a gift of her; wasn't that the symbolism? He was giving her away. The loss was quantifiable, would be even in ordinary circumstances. Fathers in movies had that shadowed look that said, My daughter's grown up; I'm old.

At least she was marrying a good man. Ben liked William, though Ben felt stilted with him. A molecular biologist, William was an expert on a tiny worm, invisible to the eye, called C-elegans. Once he'd shown Ben a photo of the worm, magnified five hundred times. It looked like a bright, crooked river. "It's the first multicellular organism we mapped the whole genetic sequence of," William had told him with barely tamped pride. That conversation had made Ben like his shy future son-in-law even more. He'd pictured him, then, not as a scientist, but as some explorer, a Lewis or Clark.

"No kidding, you've mapped the whole thing?" Ben asked.

"Not me," William said. Then he added, hesitatingly: "Well, they've mapped ninety percent of it. But that's good enough; that's really the same as all of it, in scientific terms."

No. Ten percent changes everything. Ten percent will screw you in the end. But Ben hadn't said this, not wanting to disrupt this conversation with his future son-in-law, who, if shy, if a little dorky, was still so much better than the others. There was a period in Edith's life when it seemed that she only dated married men, one doctor in particular when she was doing her third-year rotations, who made Edith call home, crying. Never to him, but he would sit by Miriam in bed, twisting the sheets, while Miriam scolded and soothed. And when his wife hung up, he said, "She's beautiful and funny and smart. Why does she put up with this crap? What kind of man—" and was made silent, then, by Miriam's hard, hot look.

"Yes, what kind of man?" she repeated, taunting him. Then, more gently: "It's familiar to her. It's what she knows."

Years ago he'd cheated, and they both knew it. In that mother-daughter way, they had consultations over the kitchen table. More than once Ben entered the room and realized he was interrupting some feminine hatching (like a hen house, he'd thought: warm, oppressive, the weight of straw). When Edith was sixteen, he'd almost left. And then, instead of giving up Miriam, his family, he gave up the woman instead; gave up all future women, all ramblings. Miriam took him back but had withdrawn, somehow. She held back a part of herself that waited and watched, in the overhang of her sharp and penetrating eyes. And Ben had accepted that, that he'd sacrificed his wife's confidence, but might win it back, with good behavior, over the years. With perseverance.

☾

In his and Miriam's bedroom, he helped William with his cuff links. They were mother-of-pearl and cut like lotus blossoms. The tuxedo buttons matched: pale, glinting shards of shell. William was nervous, and who could blame him? Shifting his weight from foot to foot, catching glances of himself in their tinted antique mirror, not seeming to recognize his reflection.

"They say weddings are harder on the grooms," Ben told him. "Brides get their nervousness out of the way beforehand."

William smiled. "Right."

"There," Ben said. "You're all linked. You're ready for linking."

"OK." William took a steadying breath. "So, any fatherly advice? I should say, father-in-lawly?"

"Yes. Deserve her."

William flinched.

"Sorry. I didn't mean it that way." William had intended his request for advice as a joke, of course; filling time and air. Their relationship had always been characterized by a kind of levity. Ben paused, trying to clarify. "Of course you deserve her. What I meant was, don't take her for granted. It takes work. You shouldn't forget that." He stopped, annoyed with himself for speaking in clichés.

William nodded. "Right. Well, I'm glad Edith and I will have you two to look toward for secrets to a long marriage."

Ben turned away. The secret to a long marriage, he might have said, is that there are always secrets. When you two go on your honeymoon, we're splitting up. That's our secret. When you two are lying on some Caribbean beach, drinking your umbrella drinks, Mimi is going to leave me. She's going to move twelve miles down the road to be with a man named Lester. They're going to grow old together, yes, and all of that. Haven't you noticed her putting away those boxes your wedding presents have come in? Didn't you see her face when Edith tried to put them in the recycling bin? Don't you see? She's been sleeping in the guest room down the hall all summer. This connubial bliss, it's all for show. Our last joint performance. I am unqualified to give advice. Disqualified, I should say.

"You look great," Ben said instead. "Dignified." He stood up. "Shall we?"

☾

Strange: In these last two months, since Miriam told him she was leaving him, they'd gotten along better than they had in years. As if a tension had lifted, had blown away. Miriam's disappointment in him, the constant work it took to please her—marriages take work, that at least was true, the truest thing he knew—all that was cleared away.

At first he'd hated the pretense of it, the artificial deadline of Edith's wedding: D-day, he called it. Miriam had insisted on it, claiming she'd take full responsibility for the fallout. "Edie will be furious, of course, that we didn't tell her in advance," she said. "But in the end, she'll be grateful, even if she doesn't admit it, or even realize it. Separating now would screw up the whole wedding. Believe me, it's what everyone would be talking about. And they'd all be watching us, when they should be attending to her. I have enough to be dealing with already without all that drama. Anyway, she'll be mad at me, not you, so don't you worry." She emphasized the "you," implying she was, once again, taking some bothersome parental chore off Ben's hands, like going to a teacher's meeting to contend with anal, blotchy Miss Chenowitz.

Now, Ben was grateful. It was like when he'd quit smoking: not all at once, but cutting back a cigarette a week, stretching out the process of withdrawal over some five months. Miriam had moved into the guest bedroom the night she told him, but other things had flowed in to fill her absence in his bed. Even their physical relationship had not completely ended. They still kissed. On walks, Miriam's bird-glasses dangling on a cord around her neck, they held hands. They were as sexual, Ben joked, as a Fundamentalist Christian couple. Mostly, though, it was the talking that kept Ben from feeling angry or desperate, that kept him something oddly close to happy, though of course he knew how thin that veneer of happiness was, how fragile the membrane that kept out the world.

He had always hated what he called those "state of the union" conversations, perhaps because they were always full of complaint. Now, he solicited them, he began them. "You only want to talk about us," Miriam said wryly, "when there is no more us." But her exasperation wasn't sincere. He could tell from the way she would settle herself in her chair, tucking her feet under her. She had, after all, thirty-five years of stored up things to say.

"Men tend to be more satisfied in marriage than women," she told him one night.

"Is that because women give more?" asked Ben. "Or because they demand more?"

It was the kind of comment that would once have enraged her, but now she laughed. The flash floods of her temper were smooth these days; she was calm as a monk. "Huh. I don't know. Probably both."

With no motivation to court him, change him, complete him, it was truth that Miriam was after.

In response to a question Ben asked her, she shook her head. "No, I know that's what you think, but it's not true. Lester was never about payback." She paused, squinting, as if the truth of it were something visible, a tree on the horizon. "Or rather, it's not as simple an equation as that, an eye for an eye."

"Or whatever body part."

She raised an eyebrow. "Or whatever. Don't bait me, Pot." (Shorthand for "pot calling the kettle black": It was her name for Ben at such moments.) "I suppose if there's a connection, it's this. Ever since that time, that last one, it's as if whatever reservoirs of goodwill and forgiveness I had for you, that we all have for the people we love, it's as if they were drained. I didn't cut you any slack anymore, I was hard on you, I wasn't generous or gracious. No…"—her hand raised like a traffic cop—"you don't have to deny it, it's true. I was always waiting for you to screw up again. 'One more time, and that's it,' was what I told myself."

"But I didn't."

"But you didn't. I believe you." A quiet, then; she looked at him sadly.

"Good," Ben said, meaning it. "I wasn't sure if you did."

She nodded. "So, where Lester comes in: Well, when I began having feelings for him, it was as if this dissatisfaction I felt, this anxiety, was something I could finally identify. I realized that I'd been waiting for you to fuck up, not so much out of paranoia or insecurity, but because it would give me an excuse to go." Her eyes widened, as if she were half-surprised at what she was saying. "You know, you need that in a marriage, those reservoirs. There was something—I guess the word for it would be parched—about you and me. And I couldn't change it. I could see you trying to make it up to me, but it's as if the pipes were shut off, and I couldn't fill those reservoirs again." She laughed. "To beat this analogy into the dust."

"It's a good analogy," Ben said. He tried to picture their marriage as Miriam saw it: something dry and spherical, like the moon, cratered. "It makes me think of that expression, 'water under the bridge.'"

"I always liked that idiom. Poetic, don't you think?"

"Well, doesn't it seem—" He leaned forward, as if he were trying to catch something, or reach it. "Doesn't it seem to you, that in the last month, we've become hydrated again somehow? Not so—what did you call it—'parched'?"

She hesitated. "Yes, I know what you mean. But isn't the point—." Her light fingers clasped his, then, as if to soften her words. "Isn't the point that the water is *under*? That it can flow again, because it's below or behind us now?"

Conversations like this hurt Ben, but there was a welcome in it, too, a pleasure that wasn't, as Miriam sometimes wondered aloud, masochistic. He felt like those Indian monks who in the process of giving things up—food, sex, pleasure—find something as basic as light. He loved her more, perhaps, than he ever had.

"This is so you," she said to him, her voice more bitter than it had been in ages. "Like when Edith had pneumonia. You're always best in times of crisis."

"But that's a good thing, isn't it?" Ben said.

"I suppose. Though I'd trade in some of that grace under pressure for more consistency." She shrugged, forced a smile. "You make it hard for me, simply by making things so easy. I should be grateful, I know."

It was a spontaneous thing to say, yet it shocked him. Should he be trying harder to keep her? Was he helping her into her coat, as it were—first one arm, then the other. Out you go, Honey, better luck next round?

It seemed to Ben that love had to be voluntary. Years before, he had felt tethered by the marriage, straining its chain. There was a world of women out there, brown legs and moist mouths, yes, but beyond that, stories he'd never heard and stories he might trade for them. Now that Miriam was leaving him, just the thought of other women exhausted him.

But how to account, then, for the relief he felt, that threaded through his sadness like veins through a leaf? He thought of a phenomenon a psychiatrist friend of theirs had once told him about: the exhilaration that happens to a worker when, fired from a job he has always liked, he clears his desk. Was that it? He wished he could remember the name of the syndrome. It obsessed him for days. Was it a disorder? A coping mechanism? Or a legitimate revelation? He wondered, but he did not, in this instance, ask Miriam.

☾

Ben could hear the sound of tires on the gravel. Fresh gravel: They'd gotten the driveway redone for the wedding, some pinkish stone. Women were funny about weddings. Look at Edith. This girl who had to be made to brush her hair for school pictures (one of the few fights she had with her mother, Ben remembered, involved a thirteen-year-old Edith informing Miriam very loudly that she did not give a rat's ass whether her damn part was straight), and all of a sudden everything had to be just so. New white and magenta snapdragons bordering the driveway, that pink gravel. He was the one who was going to have to live with it now, get the pebbles stuck in the soles of his shoes, not either of these obsessive women.

"Hey, people are arriving. Let's get a move on," Ben said.

"Hold on, Daddy. Just a couple more pictures."

"It's more caterers, I bet," Miriam said.

"Are you kidding? How many caterers are there?"

"A hundred and seven." Miriam grinned. "No, you know who I bet it is: Lucille Phegan. That woman comes early to everything."

"Mom, you were supposed to give her a special invitation saying the wedding was at six," Edith said. "Now come on, you two, focus. We don't have much time. Or actually"—this to the photographer—"you focus, Peter. What now?"

The photographer was a friend of William's, blond and bearded. He looked like Jesus Christ. Ben hoped the pictures weren't awful. There were few things he liked less than posing for pictures. Looking through vacation photos, he would complain that there were none of him. To this, Miriam would shake her head and point out the correlation between agreeing to have pictures taken of oneself and having pictures of oneself. He smiled, remembering how annoyed she would get.

"You with your parents," said Peter, finally, this Jesus of few words.

"Oh, stop your kvetching," Miriam said to Ben, but it was a preemptive scold: Ben was stilled by the thought that this could be the last picture of the three of them. Surely not? He felt something round and hard in his chest: a plastic ball. No, there would be graduation pictures with the grandchildren. He imagined Miriam and himself, twenty or so years from now, wizened and spotted, long past all silly, obstructive desires. And he and Miriam would always be friendly, that was a given. They would not be the kind of divorced parents one needed to keep at opposite ends of a lawn. No reason they couldn't both attend Christmases or Thanksgivings, birthday parties, all those photo ops. The ball expanded and broke. Peter said, "Now, the bride and her mother," and Ben was left with a suspicion that Peter had snapped him looking like a befuddled monkey.

He stood next to Peter and watched the two women in his life arrange themselves. A piece of Edith's hair had escaped her complicated, slicked-back updo. In the end Edith had opted for flowers in her hair (nature and fertility) over a veil (antiquated patriarchal tradition). There was something shiny and lacquered about her, Ben thought, appraising. He wasn't used to seeing her wear all this makeup. He preferred the way Miriam looked, still like herself. "Edith's hair—," Ben said, but Miriam was already tucking the strand behind Edith's ear.

"That's it. Look at each other, like that," Peter directed.

What was this picture for, Ben wondered. Was this standard, to take pictures of just the mother and the bride, and leave the father out like this? It seemed exclusionary. It reminded one of the mother being pregnant and self-contained, and the father incidental. Or had Miriam cooked this up? Was she thinking ahead to the picture on her desk, she and her daughter, smiling at each other (the tenderness of that look), no Ben, no fake family to spoil the shot? A picture more appropriate for her home with Lester.

"All right, father and bride, last picture."

Ben gave himself an actual shake (so clearly a standard shot: no self-pity now, no conspiracy theories, no more wallowing) and stepped up to take Miriam's smiling, lingering place.

Now they could all hear the sound of tires.

☾

Walking down the aisle, Edith on his arm: the weight of her. She whispered to him, "Slower, Daddy," and he slowed his pace. They stopped at the wooden floor.

The Unitarian minister, imported from Boston, said, "Who gives this woman away?"

"Her mother and I do," Ben said. He helped Edith climb the step. She hooked her train on her arm. Ben hesitated. From behind him, Miriam whispered, "Here," and he sat by his wife in the empty folding chair.

Ben's concentration went in and out, a bird in a house.

"Edith and William have a friend, Laura Crenshaw, who will now read a poem, Shakespeare's Sonnet 116," said the minister.

Laura stepped forward in a flutter of yellow silk. Ben thought again of those sleepovers, Laura's nightgowns, and her pair—but he could be inventing this—of pale, feathery slippers. The girls making popcorn, trying to be quiet but failing; listening to them giggling while Miriam slept beside him.

Laura took a breath and began to recite. "Let me not to the marriage of true minds admit impediments. Love is not love which alters—."

Miriam, next to him, reached over and gripped his hand. He squeezed it, then: their code from when they were nearly children, just starting out. Four squeezes, like the pulses of a heart: Who. Do. You. Love?

She hesitated, then squeezed back: I. Love. You.

How. Much?

As young lovers, that final squeeze had been bone-crush-ing, intended to make him laugh and gasp. It was still firm, though it caused no physical pain.

THE MOON CITY SHORT FICTION AWARD

2017
Kim Magowan
Undoing

2016
Michelle Ross
There's So Much They Haven't Told You

2015
Laura Hendrix Ezell
A Record of Our Debts

2014
Cate McGowan
True Places Never Are

CPSIA information can be obtained
at www.ICGtesting.com
Printed in the USA
FFHW021720290119
50351095-55446FF